THINK AGAIN

A captivating compendium of
original short stories

RENEE MARIE PHILOMENA THÉRÈSE KRAY

• • •
1

Illustrations by Lizzi Peters

Cover by Jeremy Jayme

Contents:

FIRST LOVE

She first saw him as she walked into a cafe on Second Street. The wind was blowing the leaves around in circles outside, and it seemed to push her right through the door. Later she would wonder if it had really been the wind, or if it had been the hand of fate.

A peppy French tune was playing over the radio, filling the building as thoroughly as the scent of roasted coffee that emanated from behind the counter. She took her pale blue scarf from her head, revealing her tousled hair as she eyed the patrons in the shop. Her gaze turned to the workers behind the counter.

That's when she saw him.

The beautiful French words suddenly faded into the background as she breathlessly watched him. She felt as if she were in a dream, or perhaps a wonderful movie. He was tall and thin, barely older than twenty, with sandy brown hair and hazel eyes. Stubble adorned his chin, framing a perfect smile made up of uniform white teeth.

She went towards him, drawn helplessly. Her heart started pounding and her hands began to shake as she took her place at the end of the line, never removing her eyes from his face. What should she say to him? How should she say it? After all, she had been dreaming of this moment for so long. It had to be perfect. He was the one.

* * *

She didn't need to see any pieces of documentation or ask for a test. She somehow already knew that it was him, the son from an unforeseen pregnancy, the baby that she had given up when she was only seventeen.

The background song changed into one sung by a woman. The vocals were gentle and loving, thoroughly illustrating the sentiments that she felt rising up in her heart. He looked exactly the way that she had imagined him to: perfect. A miracle.

Her miracle.

The line moved forward, towards the counter, and she moved with it. Closer to him. She felt her heart pound even harder as she looked at him and imagined being able to hug him; to tell him that she was his mother and that she had been looking for him almost since the very day that she'd given him up. She'd never guessed that the long awaited moment would happen here, at a coffee shop in an outdoor mall. She hadn't even planned on doing any shopping while on this business trip, in a strange town and state. Why had she stopped here on her way home from the meeting? Was this moment predestined? She looked back up at him as he ran a credit card through the machine, handed it back to a man, and then gave the appropriate sized cup to the girl who was making the coffees.

She suddenly wondered what his name was, and what hobbies he had. Was he in school? Belong to any sports groups? Have a girlfriend? She pictured taking him out to dinner and getting caught up on everything that she had missed in his life. Would she be able to see him get married? Welcome grandchildren into the world?

He smiled and thanked a customer who was standing only a few feet in front of her. She noticed how happy he looked, and she suddenly felt a pang of doubt. Why hadn't he ever tried to find her? Maybe he didn't want to know that he had a different mother, another family than the one that had raised him.

But why wouldn't he want to know? She had been searching for him so diligently, and this was at long last the end of her journey. Didn't she have a right to reveal herself to him, to claim what was her own?

Or had she lost her right on that snowy day twenty years ago, when she had brought him into the world in a dingy hospital room and then signed him away at the pressuring of her parents?

She was at the counter now. He smiled down at her, and she felt her breath stop coming. His voice, smooth and soothing, asked her how she was today and how he could help her.

You could come home with your mother! her heart screamed silently. She lost track of time for a moment as she looked up into his eyes.

The eyes of her son. Her baby. Her emotions welled up inside of her, each one fighting to be the one that would control her voice. She opened her mouth.

Whose happiness was more important?

"One tall coffee with cream, please," she said, handing him her credit card. She watched his fingers grip the edges of the card, sliding it through the cash register. She flashed back to that night, when she'd first seen him, so tiny and red and wrinkled. His hands had been so small then. Now they were bigger than hers.

"Have a nice day," he smiled, holding her card back out.

She looked up at him for a moment, expecting herself to falter. To change her mind. To point out to him how much they looked alike, and ask him if he had been adopted by any chance.

But she couldn't.

"Thanks," she replied. Reaching out towards him, she took her card back and stepped away.

THE GHOST IN THE WALLS

Little James tossed and turned in his dark bedroom, cold sweat gathering at his hairline and in the creases of his fingers. There were too many noises; too many creaking sounds. He'd never noticed them before, but earlier today when he had told his friends at school that he was going to be spending the night in his grandfather's old mansion, they'd balked.

"Don't you know? That place is haunted!" Tommy Teller had gasped. "You'll never make it out alive!"

"What are you talking about? My Grampa's house isn't haunted! I've been there tons of times and I've never seen anything."

"Well, I've heard stories," Tommy had mumbled. "A long time ago, there was a boy our age who was forced to work there. When he died, his ghost stayed in the house. They say that now it crawls around inside the walls, just waiting for someone that he can drag behind the panels with him!"

James had laughed in Tommy's face in the well-lit school hallway, but now, alone in the darkness of his Grampa's giant old house, he started to wonder if there was more truth to Tommy's story than he'd wanted to believe. The house was very big, very old, and very grey. It was the perfect place for a ghost to hide.

James curled up tighter under the thick sheets that covered his queen sized bed. He wondered what a ghost would look like. It would have to be thin, to get through those walls. He imagined that maybe it would bear a resemblance to the bog bodies that he'd seen his older brother researching for his high school project; their skin transformed into dark stretched leather while their bones slowly became jelly and melted away after years of being buried in the swamps. James pictured a particularly tall, thin bog creature dragging itself up the walls with the three teeth that remained in its mouth... slouching into James' room and waiting under the bed to grab his leg with the one good hand that remained on its demonic, dripping body...

James sat up in bed, pulling the covers around his shoulders as he screamed.

"GRAMPAAAAAAA!"

Within a few moments, footsteps echoed down the hall. James prayed that it was the sound of his Grampa, and not the bog ghost making one last desperate lunge to reach the bedroom.

The door whipped open. James jumped in fear as he saw a figure standing there: tall, in a menacing black cape, with wild hair like an evil Einstein.

"James? Are you alright?"

James exhaled deeply. The cape was only Grampa's bathrobe, and the figure in it was none other than the one he'd called.

"Grampa, please, you need to keep the ghost in the walls away from me!" James gasped. His Grampa

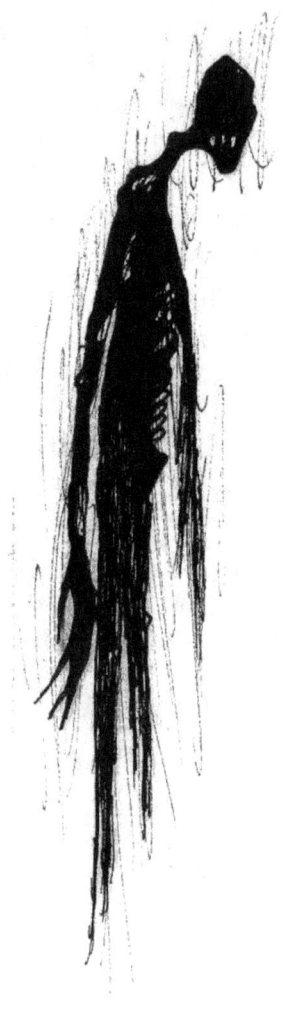

laughed, but James thought it seemed a little bit forced, not the hearty booming sound that he was used to.

"Oh, James. Were you scared? There's no ghost in this house, trust me."

"I don't believe you, Grampa," James insisted, crossing his arms tightly against his chest. He was feeling braver now that Grampa was here, and since he was being braver, he wanted the truth. "My friend Tommy was telling me earlier that he's heard the story of the ghost in the walls. I've been hearing weird noises all night. Something's here!"

James watched Grampa as he turned and looked over his shoulder, then back down at James, and then down at his shoes. Finally he sighed in defeat.

"I guess you're old enough to hear the real story," he said. He held out his hand.

James immediately climbed out of bed. The coldness of the wooden floor pierced against his skin like a million slivers, so he put on his plush orange slippers and donned the blue and green bathrobe that was hanging on the bed post. He looked like a miniature version of Grampa now. He jumped forward and grabbed Grampa's hand.

The guys at school would make fun of him if they knew that he still held Grampa's hand sometimes, but James didn't care. Those hands were rough and hard, lined with old scars that Grampa said were the illustrations to a life full of stories. James hoped that one day his hands would be full of stories, too.

Grampa led James through the old house. James couldn't help but notice the long shadows hiding between the bookshelves in the library, the creaking sound of the chandelier as it hung over the grand living room, and the multiple doors that lined the hallways and all looked eerily the same, as if he and Grampa were walking but going nowhere.

Finally they arrived at their destination: a large set of curved wooden double doors, set with golden handles that were locked tightly. James felt his eyes growing wider until they were surely bugging out of his skull, like his Aunt Lindy's pug dog. He had asked for a long time to see what was beyond the beautiful doors, but Grampa had always told him that it was very private.

"Like I said, I think you're old enough to know the truth," Grampa was saying as he fit a small golden key into the lock on the door. Grampa always wore that key on a thick chain around his neck, along with a little golden cornucopia that he said represented how blessed he was. James had always thought that the key was just a part of the necklace, not anything real.

"This is the only place that I can really tell the story right," Grampa finished as the key clicked. He swung the doors open and reached inside, turning on the lights.

James squinted, his eyes filling up with tears in a reaction to the sudden burst of light. He blinked a few times, and large patches of color slowly began to come into focus. He quickly wiped the tears away on his robe sleeve.

Then he gasped.

The room before him was a greenhouse unlike any he'd ever seen. Barrels were filled with tiny white flowers that had grown right over the edges of their vessels, like huge carpets that couldn't be contained. Four columns held up the beveled skylight window that was mounted in the ceiling, and each pillar was covered in vines that had white flowers with thick petals, twisted purple insides, and big yellow antennae-looking pieces sticking out from their centers. There were even trees, real trees that had fruit on them. James looked up at a tall one that bore small clusters of yellowing bananas. He'd never stopped to wonder where bananas came from before; he'd definitely never thought that they came from trees. In between the boxes of plants and the crates of flowers were beautiful stone statues of angels and animals.

"Isn't it lovely?" Grampa beamed with pride as he walked James through the indoor garden. "See those weird looking blossoms climbing up the poles? Those are passion flowers. And don't touch those guys in the box! They're Venus fly traps."

"They look like they have teeth!" James gasped as he examined the wide green plants, which had large spikes mounted along the outer edge of them.

"They do," Grampa explained. "They eat bugs."

"Wow," James whispered, looking at the plant with new admiration and making a mental note to tell Tommy about it when he got home.

Grampa sat down on a wide bench that was nestled between a tall potted tree and a pillar of passion flowers. James plopped down beside him, looking up at the weathered face in anticipation. Grampa hadn't just brought him here for nothing. Something important was definitely going to happen.

"Well, I promised you the truth of the matter," Grampa finally said, "and I'll give it to you. You wanted to know about the ghost in the walls, so you shall."

Fear pricked into James' spine like frozen needles.

"Is there really a ghost in the walls, Grampa?" James asked, almost afraid to hear the answer. Grampa smiled.

"Yes," he replied, "and no. Not anymore. You see, once upon a time, this was not my house. This wasn't anyone's house. This was a hotel. A very fancy one at that, I might add."

"A hotel?" James repeated. He was surprised, but at the same time it made sense. What normal house had two levels that each featured uniform doors lined evenly along the hallways?

"Yes, a small hotel," Grampa replied. "It was owned by a very nasty man whose name was Colton. No one ever called him Colton, though, they called him the Ogre. You see, Colton was a giant man, well over six feet tall, but so fat that he looked as though he had two stomachs. He never brushed his teeth and barely ever took a bath, so he smelled like sweat on top of sweat and looked like he had just rolled out of a mud pit somewhere. There was always dirt caked on the back of his neck, so much so that I think it had become a permanent part of his skin. When your mother tells you to wash behind your ears, trust me, there's a reason for it.

"Colton had inherited the hotel from his father, who had inherited it from his own father, who had built it. It was supposed to be a beautiful glimpse into the past for everyone who stayed there, an example of how life might have been if they'd lived in Victorian times. Oh, they had fancy evenings with masquerade balls down there in that living room, where everyone had to dress up formally if they wanted to get in. People came from far away to stay at this hotel. The experience was so good that there was a waiting list a mile long, and people even dealt with the disgusting Ogre in order to be able to stay at his establishment."

James could picture it all: the giant living room as a dance floor, with the crystal chandelier sparkling over all sorts of people who were decked up in beautiful dresses and suits, with masks strapped over their faces so that no one could see who was who.

"But Grampa," he asked, "if this place was such a hit, then why did it ever close down?"

"Because," Grampa explained, "of the ghost in the walls.

"You see, James, Colton was a very bad man. He wanted to have everything done right, but he also wanted it to cost him no money at all. He really was an ogre, not only because he looked like one, but because he was miserly and cheap, keeping all the money that he could for himself. He was selfish and would go to great lengths to line his own wallet, even at the expense of other people's happiness, so he was a monster on the inside as well as on the outside.

"One of his ways to get more money was to hire cheap labor to do the work of the hotel. Oh, he hired well trained adults to interact with the guests, certainly, but the hard work that went on behind the scenes, that stuff he gave to children. You see, children will work for food because that's the only way they know how to get it. So whenever the hotel needed more help in the staff, the Ogre would contact an orphanage that was nearby. The orphanage director, who was almost as much of a monster as the Ogre was, would send over some kids who were being rowdy or misbehaved so that the Ogre could straighten them out. Really what he would do was work them to the bone for almost nothing, keep them hungry most of the time, and finally break their spirits until they could see no light at the end of the tunnel; no option except to work for the Ogre obediently, doing what he said in the hopes that they might get an extra bread roll at the end of the night."

James shivered. This was sounding a lot like the story that Tommy had told him.

"That doesn't sound like straightening someone out," he said. "That just sounds like being mean."

"That's exactly it," Grampa agreed. "The Ogre was the meanest man you ever did meet. But there was one boy who actually beat him. One young man, who was only about your age when he came here, would end up getting this place closed down and end the Ogre's reign. And he did it by becoming the ghost in the walls.

"His name, before he was a ghost, had been Bernie. Bernie was always trying to escape from the orphanage, so when the Ogre needed some new workers Bernie was the first on the list to get shipped off. Along with him went his brother Jack and a young girl who was always trying to steal extra toast: little Mary Anne.

"The three kids were locked in a big crate and carried over here secretly along with all the other packages that would be delivered to the hotel, so that no one would find out about them. Those kids hammered at the sides of their wooden prison and shouted and screamed their lungs out, the same way every shipment of children did, but it was no good. No one heard them before they got to the hotel, where they were unloaded in the kitchen. They'd known that they were being taken to the hotel, as they'd heard of other kids going there before, but even knowing what was coming didn't prepare them for what they saw there.

"Inside the kitchen there was a small army of children, all workers that the Ogre kept on as his permanent staff. They were the saddest youngsters you ever did see: thin and pale, with red puffy skin around their eyes and scraggly hair pulled back from their faces by scraps of faded fabric. Bernie, Jack, and Mary Anne were immediately sent into the fold, where they were taught their duties by the other kids: wash the dishes, sweep floors at night when everyone was sleeping, wash the loads of clothes, and most important of all, NEVER get seen by any of the guests.

"Bernie, being the most rambunctious of the group, didn't intend to become one of the obedient workers for even one minute. He and Jack and Mary Anne kept each other strong in their wills throughout their time as workers, reminding each other that they didn't want to become one of the 'Sad Eyes', as they came to call the other young laborers.

"But they quickly learned that their defiance was not going to be accommodated by the Ogre. Bernie had heard stories about their new master's rage in the face of disobedience from the Sad Eyes, but he didn't discover it for himself until the first time he told the Ogre 'no'.

'No!' the Ogre had roared when Bernie told him that he would not clean the toilets that night. 'Is that what you say to me? No? Well, we'll just see about that!' "

"Did the Ogre kill him?" James whispered, white faced. "Is that how he became a ghost?"

"No, that would have been far too easy of an ending for a story. The Ogre had a special punishment that he used on rambunctious children to turn them into Sad Eyes. So he took Bernie and he locked him in the deep closet, which was where he would keep bad children, alone and in the dark, until their stubbornness broke and they sobbed like babies. Only then would he let them out, and they would never argue with him again after that.

"But Bernie was more stubborn than most of the other kids, and not to mention, he had his friends. Jack was secretly watching as the Ogre dragged Bernie off to the closet, so he figured out which wall it backed up against. Then he and Mary Anne did what none of the Sad Eyes had ever been brave enough to do: they penetrated the deep closet. They made a hole in the wall behind the closet with three knives and one spoon. Don't ask me how they got through the plaster section, but they did. And throughout Bernie's stay in the deep closet they would slip him in little nuts and tiny glasses of water so that he wasn't starving, and they'd talk to him so that he didn't feel alone. They kept his spirits up just like he'd always kept up theirs at the orphanage.

"Then came the day when the Ogre finally let Bernie out of the deep closet. He was expecting another Sad Eyes, but Bernie came out the same way he'd gone in, thanks to his friends: full of spirit. The Ogre was so mad. He raised his hand and hit Bernie across his face, so hard that Bernie fell right down onto the floor. The Ogre guessed that Bernie's friends had had something to do with the matter, too, so he stormed into the group of children, looking for Jack and Mary Anne."

"He didn't find them, did he?" James interrupted. He had his knees pulled up to his chest tightly. So far he wasn't liking his Grampa's story one bit.

"Jack had been pushed to the back of the crowd by the Sad Eyes, who all wanted to see Bernie being released," Grampa explained, "so the first person that the Ogre set eyes on was Mary Anne.

"Sweet little Mary Anne was a girl with big brown eyes and long dark hair which she always wore in two braids down the back of her head. The Ogre saw her and he roared. It was probably a yell, but they said it sounded like the rumble of an attacking animal. He lunged out and grabbed Mary Anne by one of her braids as she turned to get away, pulling her towards him. He wrapped one of his thick arms around her face so that all anyone could see of her was her eyes and her forehead. I do think he was trying to smother her in his smelly fat. But that right then is when it happened.

"Bernie pushed himself up from the ground when he saw what was going on. He wasn't going to let the Ogre hurt his friends. With a loud yell he picked up a pan that was lying in the sink and smashed it against the back of the Ogre's knees. Stale oatmeal went flying through the air along with the Ogre as he dropped Mary Anne and crashed forward, onto his face.

"But there was no time to celebrate. The Ogre was getting back up almost as soon as he had hit the floor. Now he had no thoughts for Jack or Mary Anne or any of the Sad Eyes that were surrounding him. Now he

saw only one child: Bernie, the only worker who had ever dared to defy him. Bernie took off, pushing his way through the kitchen doors with the Ogre right behind him.

"It was a terrifying chase, with Bernie dashing as fast as he could on his light feet while the Ogre lumbered close behind, his heavy steps crashing into the floor beneath him as he swore like a sailor. Bernie knew that the Ogre was catching up because he could smell the reek of sweat getting stronger and stronger and could hear the angry snorts as the Ogre blew his hot breath in short blasts from his thick nostrils. Bernie needed to do something soon, or else he would be the next one to be shoved under the Ogre's arm and buried in that putrid flesh until he couldn't breathe anymore. Thankfully, as he turned a corner, he saw his salvation."

"A policeman!" James guessed hopefully.

"Nope," Grampa said with a shake of his head. "Nothing nearly that helpful. What he saw ahead of him was nothing but a laundry chute."

"A what?"

"A laundry chute. Back then people had these long vertical tunnels that would connect one floor of a building with the laundry room. When their clothes were dirty, they would just throw them down the chutes so that they would land right in the wash room."

"You mean like that one that's on the upper floor at the end of the hallway?" James asked, recalling a tiny trap door in the side of one of the hallways in his Grampa's house.

"I mean exactly like that, in fact that very one," Grampa said. "But if you think you can be like the movies and jump straight down a laundry chute without breaking your neck, you'd be a fool. Bernie was no fool, so when he reached the chute he ripped open the trap door and then turned himself around, jumping in feet first. Only as he was wriggling into the chute did he see how close the Ogre was to him... just a few measly feet behind.

Bernie put his arms and legs outwards in the tunnel, pushing himself against it like a spider caught in a drain pipe. Then he vanished backwards into the darkness of the chute. Just in time, too, since the Ogre had reached the little trap door and was yanking it back open. Bernie started crawling slowly down the side of the pipe, moving first one foot, then the next, and then one hand, then the other, until he was completely out of the Ogre's reach. The Ogre was growling and cursing and ranting up above him for a while before he finally slammed the trap door shut again, locking Bernie in complete darkness except for the small patch of grey far beneath him where the chute looked down onto the wash room floor.

"You might have been thinking that Bernie would be feeling quite happy with himself at this point, having outsmarted the Ogre and all, but he actually felt more miserable than ever as he was suspended there, with his hands and feet pressed against the metal walls as hard as he could push them. He wanted to cry as the idea that he and Mary Anne had almost been killed really washed over him for the first time. But he knew he couldn't allow that. If even one of his hands or feet lost just the tiniest bit of strength, he would lose his grip and plummet straight down to the hard floor that was such a long way beneath him. He couldn't help but wonder what it would feel like to have all his bones smash at once. He hoped that if he did fall, the impact with the hard floor would just kill him right away so that he wouldn't have to feel it.

"But just when he was ready to give up, he noticed something. As he moved his right hand a tiny bit to get a better hold on the wall, he felt an empty space. He inched his fingers towards it, ever so slowly. The space was big. He managed to get all the fingers on his right hand curled around the edge of the space, and then he shifted his elbow over so that it came to rest on the bottom, which seemed to be made of the same metal as the chute. He now had one whole arm into what he quickly realized was a new tunnel, a horizontal one that he could crawl along. Maybe there was some hope yet.

"He pressed his left hand and leg hard against the side of the chute, pushing the rest of his body towards the new tunnel. He hit his head against the top of the tunnel at first, but then he got in. Finally with a huge push, he kicked off the chute wall with both feet and propelled himself onto solid ground.

"You know the old story that when people get back on solid land after some awful ordeal, they're so happy that they kiss the ground? Well that's exactly what Bernie did. He kissed that dusty old metal floor, and finally he let go of the tears that he had held up inside of him. For a few minutes he just laid there and let tears roll out of his eyes; tears that were happy and scared and sad all at once. But after a few minutes, Bernie pushed himself back up and wiped the salty water away. He knew that he had to keep going. The Ogre was still out there with Mary Anne and Jack. He couldn't let the monster hurt them. He prayed that they'd had the good sense to hide while the Ogre was gone.

"Bernie crawled forward into the dark tunnel. It was very small, and if Bernie had not been underfed for his age he probably wouldn't have been able to fit into it at all. Bernie tried not to focus on how closely the walls were pressed against him, how the metal rubbed on his back and knees with every motion that he made. The nagging fear that if he got stuck he would die right there rose up into his mind, but he forced it back. He couldn't afford to think of anything other than Jack and Mary Anne.

"Jack was only eight, a few years younger than Bernie, while Mary Anne was barely seven years old. They had always looked up to Bernie as their leader. After all, he was the oldest. He couldn't let them down now. He just couldn't. He had to keep going. He had to find a way to show everyone what the Ogre really was. To get him locked away for what he had tried to do to Mary Anne and the way he had turned all those other children into Sad Eyes.

"Those thoughts were what kept Bernie going as he crawled through the darkness. He decided that the tunnel must actually be some sort of pipe which brought heating and cooling or something like that through the building. Because the hotel was so old, who knows why it was there. Anyways. Bernie followed the pipe blindly, crawling through it wherever it went. There was one moment where he hit a block of solid wall and he felt panic rising up inside of him, because if that was the end of the tunnel, there was no way he could turn around to go back. But it was only a turn in the road. The tunnel was branching off into another section of the building.

"Finally, after what seemed like hours of hopeless crawling, Bernie saw something that he'd begun to despair of ever seeing again."

"Jack and Mary Anne!" James interjected enthusiastically. Grampa looked down at him with one eyebrow raised.

"Now how would they have gotten up into the pipe? No, think... what else was missing up there that would have been a big help to Bernie?"

James thought about it for a minute. The list seemed endless. Food? Water? Clean clothes? Suddenly he remembered the one simple thing that always seemed to make everything better when he himself was scared.

"Light!" he exclaimed. "Light would be a big help to Bernie, so that he can see where he's going!"

"You got it!" Grampa answered. "He saw a small patch of light shining up from the ground a few feet ahead of him. At first he couldn't believe it. If you go for a while without light, it seems as if your eyes must be playing tricks on you when you finally see it again. When Bernie was certain that he really was seeing a pale glow, he crawled towards it as quickly as he could.

"It ended up being a small grate that was looking down into a room. The room was dark except for the moonlight coming in through the window, which was providing the dim light that Bernie had noticed. Squinting to see through the slanted metal grate, Bernie eventually made out some suitcases lying on the floor along with a wooden dresser and the bottom corner of a bed.

"He was looking down into one of the first floor bedrooms. Of course no one had heard him crawling around up there, since it was the middle of the night and the guests were all asleep. But if only Bernie could wake one of them up, maybe they would be able to help him.

"Bernie hammered his fist as hard as he could on the floor next to the grate. The metal pipe echoed and re-echoed his pounding, sending it bouncing off into the silence of the night with a truly frightening racket. Below him, he heard the inhabitants of the room gasping while the silky sheets rustled as they sat up in bed. A lady demanded to know what that noise had been. A man replied that it was probably just someone in the next room being rowdy. Bernie couldn't allow them to write his plight off as 'rowdiness'. He put his mouth right down next to the grate and yelled:

'Hey! Hey, you! I need your help! Please help me!'

"For a minute there was no response, but as Bernie watched, he saw the couple slowly inch their way towards the grate, looking upwards with round eyes that glistened in the moonlight. Apparently Bernie's own eyes were glistening, too, because the woman started screaming:

'EYES! THERE'S SOMEONE IN THE WALLS!' and then she took off, bolting out of their room with her man right behind her. Bernie had never meant to scare them, but seeing their reaction gave him an idea. If he could get all the guests to complain enough, maybe they could get police or someone to come and investigate the place. Then they'd discover the Sad Eyes and find him in the walls, and give the Ogre what he had coming to him.

"So Bernie crawled a little bit further along the pipe, and sure enough, there was another grate looking down into the next room. The man inside had already been woken up by the lady's screaming, but Bernie soon had him out of bed and yelling 'who's there?' up towards the vent.

"Bernie kept at it for a long time, crawling forwards and backwards along that row of rooms, banging and shouting and screaming to keep anyone from sleeping. He yelled out that the hotel was not what it seemed; that Colton was really a monster who forced children to work to their deaths. To add up a little extra fright, he announced that he was the spirit of the children who had died working in that hotel, come to finally expose the truth about everything.

"After having been the one who was frightened all evening long, Bernie found it fantastically fun to be the one who was doing the scaring for a change. The ladies turned white and the men gulped nervously. Everyone was Bernie's audience, and they were definitely listening to him. But of course, you know that there was one person who wasn't going to take that lying down."

"The Ogre!" James shouted.

"That's right, the Ogre. He came running to see what all the commotion was, and you'd better believe he figured out what had happened pretty quickly.

'Calm down, everyone,' he tried to tell the guests. 'It's just a raccoon up in the rafters crawling around.' But the guests weren't stupid, and they knew that they'd heard someone talking. No one believed the Ogre for even one second, and when he refused to give them a real explanation, they began to panic. They thought that maybe this place was really haunted and they hadn't been warned. Maybe it wasn't safe to stay here at all! Three people packed their bags that night and demanded a refund from the Ogre. Bernie was happy to hear it as he crouched up there, listening through the vent. After all, the Ogre loved money more than anything. The one sure way to get him sad was to make him give some of that money back to people."

"What about the other guests in the hotel, Grampa?" James asked. "If only three people left, what did the others do? Go back to bed?"

"Of course not!" Grampa laughed. "They were far too scared and upset for that. So they called in what you wanted to put into the story instead of the laundry chute: a policeman.

"The policeman's name was Ernest E. Quack. Lots of people poked fun at him for his name and because of the way he was short and round, with no hair left on his head even though he was only forty. They laughed behind his back and called him Officer Duck, but really he was a very good man and a good police officer. So when the Ogre tried to tell him that the guests were just a little bit frightened over a raccoon that had gotten in, he didn't listen. The hotel occupants were talking about eyes in the ceiling and the voice of a sad child that was saying condemning things about the hotel owner. No raccoon, regardless of how much of a pest it may be, could do that.

"After hearing everyone's testimonies and many loud explanations from the Ogre, Officer Duck sent them all into the living room to wait while he looked around the rooms by himself. He went into the first room, where Bernie had awoken the couple, and called:

'Is there anyone up there? I'm a police officer. I can help you.' Bernie knew that the man was telling the truth because he had been listening in the entire time that the Ogre had been telling stories. Bernie crawled back to that first vent and knocked.

'Yes, I'm up here," he called down. In a few seconds he could see the shape of Officer Duck, standing underneath the vent and looking up.

'What's your name, son?' he asked.

'Bernie,' Bernie answered.

'And just what are you doing up there, Bernie?' Officer Duck continued.

'It's a long story.'

'If I help you get down, will you tell it to me?'

'That sounds great.'

"Officer Duck quickly went to the door of the room and asked for pliers and a big kitchen knife. The Ogre was trying to see into the room, repeatedly demanding whether or not the raccoon had been caught. He had a ridiculous smile on his face, as if he were trying to convince himself as well as the guests that nothing was wrong. But Officer Duck merely took the tools when they came, and shut and locked the door in the Ogre's sweating red face.

"In Officer Duck's steady hand, the kitchen knife quickly cut away a large portion of the thin ceiling tile. After that the pliers ripped open the bottom of the vent. Bernie looked down and he could see it: unobstructed space. In that second all of his limbs seemed to cramp up as he realized just how long he had been crouched down in the tiny tunnel.

'Back out with your feet first,' Officer Duck was saying. 'I'll make sure you don't fall.'

"Bernie crawled over the hole carefully, and then when it was behind him, he backed up. First he let one leg dangle down into the open air, and then the other. He felt Officer Duck put his hands around his waist, steadying him as he slowly inched himself out further.

'Okay, I've got you,' Officer Duck said. 'Let go.'

"Bernie had never been happier to let go of anything in his life. As soon as he pushed himself backwards from the pipe, Officer Duck's grip tightened, holding him up in the air for a moment before turning and setting him down on the bed.

"Bernie looked around the poshly decorated room, with its floral patterned curtains and elegant nightstands. He felt a surge of disbelief. Was this real? Was he really out of the orphanage, the kitchen of the Sad Eyes, and the tiny black pipes? Bernie wept like a baby on the inside, but his eyes couldn't make the tears come. They only stared at the colors of his new surroundings and reveled in the feeling of the soft, cool mattress cushioning his tired, dirty limbs. The bed sank down as Officer Duck seated himself beside Bernie.

'So,' he said. 'Let's hear that story.' "

"And did he tell him the story, Grampa?" James asked.

"He most certainly did, exactly the way I just told you. After Officer Duck had heard all about the Sad Eyes who worked in the kitchen, the orphanage, the Ogre's attack against Mary Anne and the way he chased Bernie into the laundry chute, he was hopping mad. He got Bernie a tall glass of cold water to drink, and while Bernie was enjoying that, Officer Duck called in the backups. I wish you could have seen when they all came, with their sirens screaming and their red lights flashing through the darkness of the night. Bernie watched through the window as they put the Ogre in handcuffs, taking him away for child labor and abuse. He was screaming that it was the orphanage director's fault, but the cops told him not to worry, they were going to get that man too."

Grampa stopped and laughed. He put a hand around James' shoulders and patted him.

"But what happened to Bernie and Jack and Mary Anne, and all the Sad Eyes?" James prodded, displeased at the interruption in the story. "Were they saved?"

"You betcha!" Grampa said with a smile. "Those cops went into the kitchen and found every last one of them. They took them off to good homes with people who would care for them for a while until they felt better. Not one of them ever had to scrub carrots, peel potatoes, or wash old pans again. Bernie was reunited with Jack and Mary Anne, who, besides being worried sick about him, were just fine."

"So... it was a happy ending?" James asked tentatively. Grampa nodded. "Then how did there get to be a ghost in the walls?" he asked in amazement. "I thought that was Bernie!"

"It was," Grampa explained. "The guests who had left never found out the truth about the place, and the cops tried to keep it hushed up to protect the children from any unwanted publicity. So the people who had been in the hotel that night never knew the truth about Bernie. They went around and told everyone that there was a ghost in the walls of the building, and from there on, the rumor spread. Bernie's little act as the ghost in the walls became famous. They all thought it had been real. Bernie and Jack and Mary Anne never told anyone the truth, and neither did Officer Duck. No, they were all just glad that it was over."

• • •

"So what happened to them?" James asked.

"Well, Officer Duck went on to enjoy a long and successful career in the police force, while the Ogre enjoyed a long and unhappy stay in prison, along with his buddy the orphanage director. After the Sad Eyes were feeling better, they were all sent to a new orphanage that had a caring person in charge of it, one who gave them quality care until they were old enough to live their own lives."

"And what about Bernie?" James continued. "What happened to him?"

Grampa looked back down at James with a mysterious half smile.

"What do you think happened to Bernie, James?" he asked. James thought about it for a minute. He looked down at his Grampa's hands, and all the stories that were in them, and put his own smaller hand into one of them.

"Your name is Bernard," he said slowly. "Grampa, are you Bernie?"

Grampa nodded.

"Yes," he replied. "Bernie and I are one and the same. That was me who went down the laundry chute, and scared those people, and helped Officer Duck stop the Ogre."

"You're the ghost in the walls," James finished. He stared at his Grampa as the man stood up. The legend that Tommy had heard, the ghost story that other people actually believed was true, was really just the man that he had admired and loved for as long as he could remember.

He was suddenly filled with a brand new respect for his older relative, a sense of awe that ballooned through him from the top of his head to the tips of his fingernails.

"I told you there was no reason to be afraid of this building," Grampa said, "and now you know why. It helped me earn my freedom, and so that's why, when I was old enough to afford it, I bought the place. People thought I was downright crazy to want to live in a small hotel, and one that was haunted to boot! But I knew the truth, and we couldn't have been happier here."

"We? You mean you and Gramma, before she died?"

"That's right, James. You only knew her as Gramma Mary, but her full name was Mary Anne."

"You married Mary Anne!" James yelled in excitement. He had only known his late grandmother as a woman who had made the best chicken noodle soup and who could spell any word that he asked her about. He'd never even considered the idea that in her youth, she had survived an attack from an Ogre.

"I most certainly did marry her," Grampa said as he led James back towards the great wooden double doors, opening them up so that James could once again see the hallway of the grey hotel in front of them. "We made this place, once our dungeon, into our palace. This room used to be the Ogre's office. Now it's a space for plants to grow, making beautiful the area that was once ugly, bringing color where before there was only grey shadows. Jack helped us set it up. You don't remember your Great Uncle Jack, but he became a landscape artist after we escaped from the Ogre's clutches. He married your Great Auntie Emma, who had been one of the Sad Eyes when we first came here."

James hung on every word his Grampa said as they headed back down the hallways. He could practically see Grampa as a boy his own age, dashing through the passageways with the Ogre close behind. He only came back to the present moment when they reached his bedroom door.

Grampa opened it and led James inside. James kicked off his slippers, clambered onto the mattress, and slid back under the covers. When he was all situated, Grampa stopped for a moment beside him.

"Still scared?" he asked.

"Nope," James replied with a smile. "I'll never be afraid of the ghost in the walls again. After all, I love that ghost."

Grampa ruffled his hair with a chuckle.

"Good. Because he loves you, too."

"Goodnight, Grampa."

"Goodnight, James."

LOVE IS BLIND

There was no way that she deserved someone as beautiful as him.

Marie was just a simple girl from an even simpler town, despite the fact that she didn't look the part. She was blessed with wide dark eyes and curling black hair; fair marble skin and slender limbs. However her level head never allowed her to use looks to her advantage, as she knew that it was what was on the inside that counted, not the outside. That was probably why she was able to see the worth inside of him even when he himself couldn't.

He was a down-on-his luck lawyer who'd fallen onto bad times financially, with no friends or supporters to speak of besides his dog. She'd first been introduced to him when his sister, one of her nursing co-workers, had taken her along to his house. Apparently the distraught man had tried to commit suicide, and the sister had her hands more than full as it was. She needed someone to help her. Just a half an hour a week, check up on him, chat with him, make sure he was taking the proper medications. It was simple; an easy favor for a friend. But it quickly became more than just another medical case.

Marie tried to remember back to the exact moment that she had fallen for him, but it was hard to tell. Maybe she'd loved him since that first second when she'd walked into his modest suburban home and had seen him standing there... so lost, so confused, but so beautiful. There was an honesty that clung to him; a sense of realness that she didn't normally see emanating from other people. She tried her best to make him see it, too: that his desire to be himself and live a life he was honestly pleased with was not something that he should be ashamed of. Trying to make his dream life a reality could make things frustrating, certainly, but that didn't mean that existence could never be worth anything. She didn't have words to properly express to him that simply by living, he had already given her own life a new sense of worth, of purpose.

Of love.

As both a nurse and as a woman in love, there was nothing that gave her greater joy than to see him slowly reclaiming his life, finding new pleasure in the day-to-day activities that had formerly distressed him to the point of trying to end himself. He stood up to the people who had previously frightened him, and discovered that he was strong. He started to break through the confusion about his life, and realized that purpose could be found in simply being himself. It brought a thrill to her heart every time she saw him smile. They had only that half-hour session every Thursday evening, but she would take what she could get. What did it matter how much or how little they were allowed to be together? She was in love, the type of love that was real and deep.

She knew because she'd been in love before.

Her first husband had been a wonderful man, and when he'd died from a heart attack years ago, she hadn't thought that she would ever be able to love again. But now here was her patient, her beautifully breathtaking patient, who both needed to be saved and was doing the saving. She supported him as he reclaimed his life; he infused hers with the beautiful jewel of knowing that she had a purpose. She was able to love again, and he was able to live again. They were meant to be together.

Every week after their session was over she would bid him goodbye and leave with more than half of her mind fighting to turn her body around. It whispered that she should run back, hammer on the door, and tell him everything that she was feeling: how they were perfect together. She often fantasized that he would accept her declaration of love and return it with one of his own. That he would wrap her pale, slender young body in his toned arms and hold her close to his chest. The muscles in his torso were always just barely visible beneath the thin grey t-shirts that he favored. Every time she saw him it made her even more attracted to him, made her want desperately to touch him.

But she never did.

How could she tell a professional client that she'd fallen for his quirky but delightful personality without driving him away? That she melted each time she saw his deep blue eyes without sounding bubble-gummy? How might she possibly make him understand that his life had quite suddenly affected hers in such a deep way that she felt like a better person simply for having known him?

Marie couldn't think of a single way to do it, to tell him everything and make him not only hear it but also feel it. To try to tell him her feelings before he was ready would jeopardize everything. He was still recovering from his depression and attempted suicide. It would overwhelm him now if she were to tell him the truth. He only really knew her as a nurse, one of many that he had seen in his life, and until he could see her as more than just one of the crowd she couldn't risk telling him how he had become so much more to her. So every week after their visit she would allow her mental fantasies to run wild while she herself turned her back on him with an orderly step. Marie could wait.

He was worth waiting for.

...*...

"Marie? Marie, are you ready for dinner?" The man who had spoken reached out and touched the shoulder of the woman sitting in front of him. She gave no answer, her eyes simply stared straight ahead the way that they always did. Kevin looked up to the glowing box in front of her, where a television show was playing out on the screen. She never missed the new episodes or the reruns; she watched the show religiously. He didn't even know what it was really about, but he'd seen snatches of it before when he came to get Marie.

Some sitcom based around a confused lawyer and his dog.

"Come on, Marie," Kevin, who was clad in dark red scrubs, said again. "The show is ending. We have to get you to the dining room. Ed and I are going to help you walk there. Okay?" Ed, another male nurse who was standing nearby, walked over and put his hand underneath her elbow. Between the two of them, they managed to get Marie into a standing position. She moaned under her breath and looked back towards the TV.

"Why does she love that show so much?" Ed asked. "It's just television."

"I don't know. She just does," Kevin shrugged. "You only started working here a month ago so you didn't see it, but after Marie's husband passed away three years ago, she went downhill fast. We didn't think she was going to make it much past him. But suddenly she just hooked on to this show, and then she started getting better. It's the only thing that keeps her quiet now. We even had to get the DVD to play for her when the seasons end."

Ed looked at the frail old woman who was hobbling slowly between them. He imagined that she had probably been a great beauty at one time, maybe with wide dark eyes and curling black hair; fair marble skin and slender limbs. But now she was ninety-five, hunchbacked, and covered in sagging skin that was turning leathery from years of exposure to the world. Her eyes looked around her surroundings dully, obviously not processing where she was or who was helping her. Several times he saw her glance over her shoulder towards the common room of the retirement home, which was where the television was located.

"So, Marie," Ed said to her, moving his head so that his face was in her line of vision. "Why *do* you like that show so much?" The old woman mumbled; something about it being worth waiting for.

"I think my favorite shows are worth waiting for, too," Ed said under his breath to his co-worker as he straightened back up, "but I'd never get this crazy over any of them."

"Me neither," Kevin agreed. "I guess you never know what can affect people, but it does seem a little extreme."

"Yeah. After all, it's just another TV show, right?"

EMPLOYEE OF THE MONTH

Nothing unusual ever happened at Tinken's General Store. The same employees worked the same shifts, the same customers came in to purchase the same products, while the same dull music droned on over the loudspeaker.

Then Jim Rines didn't show up for work.

Mr. Tinken unlocked the front door with the old key partly caked with rust, the way he always did. He turned on the lights, illuminating the seven aisles that were stacked with everything from pre-packaged food to cheaply made toys. Mr. Tinken adjusted the heat on the dial beside the door, setting it to a toasty 52 degrees. Mr. Tinken hated setting the heat at all, because it was a useless waste of money. His employees would complain the same as they did every day about how it needed to be higher, but Mr. Tinken thought that 52 degrees was already too much.

Mr. Tinken glanced at the clock on the wall. The second hand had broken off, leaving a small jagged stump clicking steadily around the center of the clock. No one ever needed that tiny little wand, anyways; the minute and hour hands were plenty. Right now, the two and a half hands were all pointing to the same conclusion: Jim Rines was late.

Mr. Tinken and Jim Rines were neighbors. They had grown up in the same houses that they now owned, and used to play together as kids. When Mr. Tinken had bought out this old business, Jim had quit his job at the busy car wash downtown to come here and help his "ol buddy" get his business up and running. Secretly, Mr. Tinken hated being called Jim's "ol buddy." Sure they had known each other their whole lives, but Mr. Tinken *did* sign Jim's paychecks. He was the boss; he should be treated as such at all times.

In all their forty years of working together at this store, Jim had never been late before. He would always walk in through the door at exactly five minutes before nine, wearing his thick coat with the collar pulled up past his ears, his mouth parted in a wide smile that revealed his one missing front tooth as he said, "Mornin', ol' buddy." Now it was five past nine, and still there was no Jim. Mr. Tinken stared at the door in expectation. He couldn't wait to hear Jim's explanation for this.

What, the morning cold just too much for your old bones, Jim? he mused to himself. *Hurts to get out of bed? Well, you're not the only one. My doctor says that I have arthritis in both my knees, and yet here I am, right on time!*

At nine thirty the cashier came in. Her name was Florence, and Mr. Tinken had known her since his high school days. Back then she had been elegantly curved, with a slim waist and soft white skin that perfectly bore her rich chocolate eyes and waves of blonde hair. She had been the Prom Queen, the one that everyone wanted to date, to have, to love.

Mr. Tinken had asked her out that night, the evening of the last school dance, when she had looked like a vision in her ruffled red dress with the twisting silver crown mounted on her head, reflecting all the light of the twirling disco balls mounted up above them. She had scoffed at him and reminded him that she HAD a boyfriend, thank you very much, and had slid off to cling to the arm of her quarterback future husband, leaving Mr. Tinken enraged and embarrassed, with no comfort except for the "everything will be alright" pat that Jim Rines placed on his shoulder.

Now she worked for him. She had come years ago, when the business was first starting, and had begged him to give her a position. Apparently her quarterback, whom she had married young, hadn't gotten into the NFL and he didn't have many other skills beyond throwing himself at other men on the football field. They were tight on money and she needed a job.

At first Mr. Tinken had been determined to scoff at her, the same way she had scoffed at him, but Jim Rines had laid into him with a lot of jabber about being the bigger person and other pointless crap like that. At any rate, Mr. Tinken finally allowed her to take the position, partly to get Jim to shut up about it but partly because Florence still fascinated him in an unexplainable way.

She certainly was no longer the vision she had been, having gained weight in various places. She tried to hide it by wearing girdles that pulled her waist in, giving her a ridiculous V shape and making her red in the face. The redness she covered up by caking on layers of white powder and creamy makeup, and lining her eyes with any color from purple to green to orange. Her hair had gone from long butterscotch blonde to a yellow ball of wiry poof that she liked to pile on top of her head.

But she was still Florence, the Prom Queen who had turned him down all those years ago, and now she called him boss. Maybe that was what fascinated him. Maybe it was because he liked to sit in his office, staring out at her when she was busy with a customer, and imagine that she knew he was better than her now-lazy quarterback with the beer gut who worked only as a handyman on the weekends, leaving her to pay most of the bills.

He also couldn't put his finger on why he still found himself physically attracted to her, regardless of the way her looks had not held up to the test of time. His mind somehow seemed to gloss over those unflattering details, focusing on the feminine features that she still possessed and pushing everything else out of his eyes until he saw exactly what he wanted to see: the woman he'd always lusted after.

She was buttoning up her coat now instead of taking it off. He was disappointed; he wanted to see what shirt she had selected to pull on over her girdle that morning. Maybe it would be worth it to turn up the heat once in a while.... Nah, what was he thinking. Florence would always be here, money would not be.

● ● ●

"Where's Jim, boss?" she was asking him now, looking around the empty store in confusion.

"Late," Mr. Tinken growled. The bell above the door jangled, but it was not Jim walking in. It was Mitch, the young guy who worked the floors, keeping everything orderly and helping out customers if they needed it. He was late, but that was nothing new. He was always late, coming in at nine thirty-five rather than nine. He looked around in confusion, and opened his mouth to say something, but Mr. Tinken knew what it was going to be and cut him off sharply.

"Yeah, Jim's not here. He's late."

Mr. Tinken didn't mind being sharp to Mitch. If the little snob didn't do such a good job, Mr. Tinken would have fired him years ago. Mitch was only in his twenties, and worked at the store as a side job to help pay his college tuition. He had a well-shaped face with light blue eyes and sandy brown hair, plenty of it still. His body was still firm and defined, the image of a young man in his prime. Every time Mr. Tinken saw him it reminded him of everything that he had lost. He could only picture his own thinning black hairs, brushed carefully over his otherwise bald head to give the illusion of a full crop, and the fact that his skin was slowly sagging over whatever muscles he had left, hiding them from public sight.

Mr. Tinken loved to hate Mitch for his success, having not only his youth but also the great personality and loving girlfriend that Mr. Tinken had never been able to secure. That was one of the reasons that Mr. Tinken had told Mitch to come in at nine thirty-five instead of at the beginning of the hour. Even though Mitch was never really late, Mr. Tinken loved to pretend that he was, feeding the disgust he felt towards the boy. It was another private reason to hate the little perfect monster.

It was now almost ten o'clock. Soon Ms. Blochett would be waddling through the doors to get three cans of fancy feast for her white Persian cat, Mr. Blochett. Mr. Blochett insisted on going everywhere with Ms. Blochett, as she would explain the way she had every day for as long as the store had been open, and he needed his three meals to be picked up each individual morning. Bulk purchases would not satisfy Mr. Blochett.

Then, while she was paying for Mr. Blochett's selection, Elvis would come in, followed by Marilyn Manson. Those weren't their real names, but Mr. Tinken and his workers had never called them anything else, since their image influences were obviously those two music legends. One had slick black hair and a bejeweled jean jacket that he always wore regardless of the weather, while his companion sported long dark locks with pale foundation makeup, red eye shadow, and occasionally even a little splattering of lipstick. Their shopping carts always contained a hodge podge of random items, and Mr. Tinken didn't even want to ask the purpose for their selection. Usually Jim would approach them with his imperfect smile and be the one to help them out, not even

seeming to care how their appearance was so out of place.
But then again, Jim was a strange one.

This time, Elvis and Marilyn Manson were on
their own. Surprisingly, after wandering the store a few
times and being offered assistance by Mitch instead, they
left empty handed. They had never done that in all the
years that they had been coming. Mr. Tinken suddenly
wondered if maybe the reason they had been customers

for so long was because of the consideration that Jim showed them. He quickly blew the thought out of his mind. Jim was an awful worker who obviously didn't care about the company, or else he would have actually shown up to work and not played hooky.

The rest of the day passed as usual, with a few more regulars passing through the doors and making the same purchases as they had the day before. Mitch complained again about the coldness of the building and suggested that they might get more customers if the store didn't have such a reputation for being uncomfortably freezing inside. Mr. Tinken rolled his eyes and sarcastically said he would take his thoughts into consideration, secretly planning to set the thermometer to fifty-one degrees tomorrow, just to show Mitch. Mitch the whining bitch. Mr. Tinken grinned and congratulated himself silently on his wit with words.

By the time the store was completely empty and the "open" sign had been switched to "closed", Jim had still never set one foot inside the building. The employees were waiting outside as Mr. Tinken closed the door and locked it behind him.

"You gonna check up on Jim?" Florence asked as she stepped off the curb towards her car, quickly catching herself from falling as she stumbled on her stumpy black heels. Jim was disappointed. He was hoping that she could have fallen, so that he would have had the opportunity to put a hand on her waist and help her up. He would only feel the thick boned fabric of her girdle, true, but he could at least imagine the warm flesh underneath it. Mr. Tinken realized that she was now staring at him, waiting for an answer to her question. He quickly cleared his throat to make up for the awkward silence that had just passed.

"No, I'm not."

"But he's never missed a day of work before," Florence said, pulling her hair away from her face. In the flickering glow of the parking lot lights, Mr. Tinken couldn't help but notice the stress of the skin around her lips and chin where it had been pulled back in plastic surgery. He halfheartedly wondered how long it had taken her to save up for such a procedure, if money was still as tight as she'd always said it was.

"I'm just saying that maybe you should make sure he's okay, is all," Florence was continuing. "Or why don't you give me his address? I could check up on him if you wanted."

Mr. Tinken rolled his eyes and allowed an inkling of disgust to creep into him, replacing the fascination he'd felt towards her just moments before. He didn't like being preached to, especially not by the ex-prom queen who should have been his all these years.

"That's just what he wants," Mr. Tinken replied firmly. "He's probably sitting there in his old armchair, all bundled up in that raggedy robe that he wears on Sundays when he goes to get his paper, just waiting for me to knock on his door and tell him how much he was missed. Well, no go. He cost us money today by loafing.

He doesn't deserve any further consideration beyond keeping his job."

Mr. Tinken firmly blocked out the mumbled conversation that was continuing on between his workers as they wondered where Jim could be and hoped that he was alright. He stepped towards his car, holding his chipped keychain up. It was an old gift that his grandmother had given him years ago: a penny encased in a thick plastic circle that bore the words "As long as you have a penny, you'll never be broke!" Mr. Tinken thought it was cheesy, but he didn't like the idea of being broke at any rate. He selected a key off of the old ring and shoved it into the lock on his car door, twisting it roughly. The locks clicked back and the door opened. Mr. Tinken got into his vehicle and slammed the entrance shut behind him before putting another key into the ignition.

There was a tap on the window. Mr. Tinken glanced to the side and saw Mitch standing there, mouthing something. Probably a question about something that had to be done for the business. Mr. Tinken had had quite enough of employees for that day. He gave Mitch a sarcastic wave, ignoring whatever the boy was trying to ask, and pressed the worn handle of the gear shift forward into drive. The tires squealed against the pavement and the car zipped forward, leaving Mitch to jump aside.

Once he'd driven the fifteen boring minutes on the cracked pavement road to get to his house, Mr. Tinken pulled sharply into the driveway and cut the engine. His property was squashed between two others, one of which he turned away from in disgust. Jim's house. He refused to look at it; refused to give its inhabitant the pleasure of a single thought. Instead, he focused on his own abode.

His home, unlike his store, would be warm at seventy-six degrees. He himself had set the thermometer to that number when the first cold day had rolled around for the year, and it had stayed that way ever since. Mr. Tinken didn't mind paying for heat in his own home. That was an investment. After all, keeping the house comfortable was essential to a good night's sleep. And a good night's sleep was essential to having good dreams. Maybe even the best dreams, the ones where he was young again, and was playing the famed part of the school quarterback who had just saved the game.

The lights would be bright in his eyes, while the cheerleaders jumped and squealed in their tight, thin outfits, screaming his name. The cheerleaders at his school had never dressed the way the modern ones did, but that was the point of the dream: everything was just as Mr. Tinken wanted it. They'd also never known his name, and he'd never experienced the finale of the fantasy, either... Florence, pale and young as she had been, with red lips and flowing blonde hair that wasn't covering up any surgery lines, running out towards him in the glittering white dress she'd worn for graduation, while the crown on her head was brighter and more brilliant than all of the stadium lights combined.

That was usually the part where he woke up.

Mr. Tinken finally got out of his car to face the cold of the outside world. He slammed the car door behind him roughly and took a heavy step towards his front porch.

"Hey!" a voice called. Mr. Tinken stopped, grinding his teeth. He knew who it was.

"Edith," he acknowledged, blandly staring across the picket fence that separated their yards. Edith, the neighbor on the other side of his house, was waving a mittened hand to him in greeting. She was a girl that he had met at community college in the one semester he had attended. She had been a splash of color and frizz, an embodiment of friction that could not quite smooth in with the rest of the world around her. Wiry auburn hair, braces, and thick black coke glasses offset the rainbow striped gloves and legwarmers that she always seemed to pair with each outfit. The very memory of the ridiculousness could still make Mr. Tinken chuckle. What a fool.

The legwarmers had gone, but Edith's taste for color seemingly hadn't. Her house was the only one on their street not colored grey or white, being a surprising shade of lilac purple. She liked to pair knee length dresses with tights and slipper boots, which even Mr. Tinken had to begrudgingly admit suited her thin body well. Even so, he wondered what she was trying to prove, dressing like a young person and all. That wouldn't change the fact that really, she was old. Just as old as he was. She had retired from her job as a teacher and now lived alone in her ridiculously colored building with her three little dogs. A crazy red haired lady in her purple house. That's all she was.

"How's the business going?" Edith was asking. Mr. Tinken shrugged his shoulders, refusing to give her the pleasure of a response as he turned through the four keys on his ring over and over again, pretending to be resolutely searching for the one that would open his front door.

"It's cold out," Edith continued, more to the small dog that was sniffing the ground at her feet than to anyone else. She looked back up at Mr. Tinken. "Do you want to come in for a mug of hot tea, or something? I just made some."

Great. Herbal tea made by Friction Edith. That was the last thing that Mr. Tinken felt like "enjoying".

"I gotta get some stuff ready for tomorrow," he lied as he took another step towards his house, quicker this time. Edith was replying something as he shoved his key into the lock, probably some useless drabble about how it was nice to see him, hope to talk to him again sometime, blah blah blah. He got inside and closed the door in the middle of her sentence.

The heat enveloped him like a comforting blanket, seeping through every pore of his body. He let his limbs relax, absorbing the warm as he walked past his empty kitchen with the one shabby folding chair set at a rickety plastic table. The cereal bowl from that morning's breakfast still sat there, but he had no urge to clean it up.

Mr. Tinken didn't even bother to turn on the lights, because what was there to see anyways? All the walls in his house were bare. Mr. Tinken felt that art was a waste of money, and he didn't have any pictures that were worth the trouble of framing.

He opened up the door to his room, grabbing the pajamas which were still lying in a crumpled heap on his bed. He pulled his work shirt off from over his head and donned the soft flannel button-up shirt instead. Mr. Tinken always changed in the dark. He preferred not to see his body, so that he would not be reminded of how much he had let himself go. No, not let go. How much of his youth that time had taken from him. That was more like it.

Mr. Tinken got into bed, even though it wasn't yet eight o'clock in the evening. He stared out the window that was on the left side of his room. The winter sun had set hours ago, and there were no stars to peek through the blackened sky. The only light left was from the lamppost that marked the property line between Mr. Tinken's house and Jim's.

Jim Rines. Why had he not shown up for work that day? The question burned in Mr. Tinken's mind. In the store, he had been certain that it was just an attempt to loaf off so that the old fool could get some attention. He'd always been jealous of the way that it was Mr. Tinken who owned the business, while he, Jim, did nothing except help out the occasional customer and unload stock from the back rooms. Jealous. Green with envy. He'd always been that way.

Hadn't he?

Now, in the silence of his empty house, Mr. Tinken began to wonder if maybe it was something else besides an all-consuming desire for attention that had driven Jim to deliberately miss work. Could he have found another job?

Did he finally take up the offer of that annoying twit who managed the huge twenty-four hour supermarket down the road, nearly driving Mr. Tinken out of business, and who only came to the store to ask Jim to come work for him instead? That idiot, with his rail thin body, dirt brown suit, and ugly checkered tie; he tried so hard to be all prim and proper.

The more Mr. Tinken thought about it, the more the idea seemed to make sense. Jim Rines wasn't being lazy, he was being a traitor! After all those years Mr. Tinken had paid his salary, he had bowed out without a single sense of loyalty.

Mr. Tinken examined the small square home visible through his window, outlined faintly in the light of the lamp. His business and his checks had paid for the upkeep on that house for years. He had kept Jim's pantry stocked and paid for all his expenses, only to have him switch jobs the moment the opportunity was right! What a joke his "ol buddy" had turned out to be. Mr. Tinken turned over on his side, facing away from the window and the silhouette of Jim's house. Mr. Tinken was determined not to think about Jim anymore. He wouldn't give him the pleasure of the attention.

The next morning Mr. Tinken pretended not to be surprised when Jim didn't show up again. It figured, after all. If he were to walk right down to that fancy-shmancy supermarket, he'd probably see Jim standing behind the counter. Well, two could play at that game.

It was a known fact that the manager of that supermarket mostly hired people as seasonal help when the holidays came around. Therefore, in just a little while, Jim's new job would be obliterated and he'd be left penniless, unless he came crawling back. And he would. When that happened, Mr. Tinken would be waiting for him.

Later that day, the delivery of restocks arrived. It was a collection of cardboard boxes of all different sizes and weights, piled high on a flat wooden pallet and wrapped in multiple layers of clingy clear plastic like a clod of twisted cotton candy from a carnival gone wrong. It had always been Jim's job to cut through the sticky plastic wrap and open the boxes, sorting them into the different departments where they would be placed out for sale on the shelves. He used to do it all by himself, but as the business became better and he became older, Jim had begun asking Mr. Tinken to hire someone to help him manage the floor during the day so that he could spend more time with the freight in the back. And because Mr. Tinken was a considerate owner, he had agreed and hired Mitch.

Now Jim wasn't there to start unpacking the new load. Mr. Tinken looked up at the massive crate of plastic and cardboard, which seemed to tower over his five-foot-five frame even higher than usual. He picked up the knife that Jim used to use for just this purpose and began to rake it across the thick layers of white cocooning. The first layer of the plastic separated in a thin line, revealing another layer exactly like it underneath.

Mr. Tinken growled in disgust and threw the knife down, watching it clatter across the cement floor before sliding into a corner. Why should he have to do this? Business managers don't have to deal with things like unpacking and unrolling and breaking down crates. That was Jim's job. Just because he had slunk off didn't mean that he should be able to come back scotch free. This would be waiting for him when he got back.

The next day passed equally uneventfully. Elvis and Marilyn came in again, but stayed even less time than they had before. The day after that came and went and still no Jim. Mr. Tinken closed the blinds on his bedroom window so that he wouldn't have to see Jim's house and be forced to think about where the old fool could possibly be. Mitch and Florence whispered between themselves about where Jim could have gone, but seemed to have the good sense to shut their ridiculous traps whenever Mr. Tinken walked up. However, he heard snatches of their conversation every now and then.

Apparently Florence had called his house several times and had gotten no answer. Mitch, who had been told by Jim about his and Mr. Tinken's neighborhood, had gone there, figured out which house was Jim's, and knocked on all the doors and windows. Everything was locked and no one answered.

Maybe, they speculated, Jim had retired and moved somewhere warm and tropical. Maybe he'd been called out of town on a family emergency. Maybe he'd gotten tired of the way that Mr. Tinken gave him no credit for how he'd helped build the company from the ground up and had finally just moved on to somewhere that he would be more appreciated.

Mr. Tinken hated that last idea. He, Mr. Tinken, had built this place into a beautiful establishment from absolutely nothing, not stupid old Jim. He knew the truth of the matter. Jim had just decided to back stab all of them by taking some fancy new job. That was it. That had to be it.

Shortly after the first week had passed, Mr. Tinken received the first non-temperature related complaint that he'd had in a long time. Ms. Blochett had stormed up to him, wobbling dangerously in her pointed black boots, and clutching Mr. Blochett with chubby fingers that quivered in anger.

"You are out of the tuna and beef meal cans," she practically spat into Mr. Tinken's face. "Your supply has been dwindling for the past week! What's wrong with you? Can't you get more? Mr. Blochett is going to starve if you keep this up!" Mr. Tinken looked down at the fluffy white feline, who seemed plenty well fed to him.

"Where's Jim?" Ms. Blochett continued, her voice now squealing with anger. "Why hasn't he restocked the shelves?"

"Jim took a temporary leave of absence," Mr. Tinken replied flatly. "We don't know when he'll be back."

"Don't worry, Ms. Blochett," Mitch announced as he walked up from behind them, placing one hand comfortingly on her shoulder like a sap and using the other to stroke the top of Mr. Blochett's head. "I'll go in the back and find some new cans of food. It might take a few minutes, but I'll find the box."

Ms. Blochett's anger instantly melted into gratitude, signified by tears which welled up on the flabby lids that surrounded her tiny eyes.

"Oh thank you, Mitch," she whispered. "Mr. Blochett and I appreciate it so very much... you're such a kind boy..."

Mr. Tinken wanted to gag. What a drama queen. People were so easily bought by youth and a smile. Mitch was now bustling off to the back to try to find a box full of the slop that Ms. Blochett insisted on stuffing into her living furball. It took about five minutes for him to return, during which time Ms. Blochett followed Mr. Tinken around and drilled him with questions about Jim. Why wasn't he here anymore, where had he gone, when would he be back? Finally Mitch returned with a cardboard box that was jammed with cans. Ms. Blochett thanked him repeatedly, selected her three cans of overpriced mush, and trotted off towards the cash register to hand her purchases to Florence.

"You know," Mitch said quietly, "the crate hasn't been unpacked. And we're supposed to be getting another one in tonight."

"I know," Mr. Tinken replied. "That's Jim's job."

Mitch said nothing, but Mr. Tinken noticed that for most of the day, he was walking in between the back room and the main floor, restocking various sections of shelving that had started to thin out. Overzealous Mitch the bitch. What did he have to prove? Why did he have to stand up for Jim? It's not like he owed him anything. At any rate, work was getting done, so Mr. Tinken decided to say nothing. But if Mitch thought he would be getting a raise or some dumb associate award, he had another think coming.

The weeks dragged on as December slowly went by. Christmas came and went, the one day of the year when the store was closed. More complaints issued in, and for once, the temperature of the building was the last thing to be mentioned. The harsh words were all about how few items the store had in stock, how there was never anyone available to help the customers out (because manic Mitch just HAD to be in the back room unloading shipments), and of course the absence of Jim.

Mr. Tinken honestly wondered why people cared so much. Jim was just one worker; he didn't represent the entire store. Why did people care whether or not he was there to say, "Good mornin' to ya!" through his broken smile? Yet people did. They asked about the moronic old bat almost every day. Elvis and Marilyn stopped coming altogether when Mr. Tinken finally told them that their so-called friend was gone for an undetermined period of time.

Mitch became even more of a bitch, complaining that he couldn't keep up on stock while also being the only available associate to manage the floor. Florence offered to help customers out and restock the shelves when it wasn't busy, which it rarely was, but Mr. Tinken would have none of that. She was a cashier, damn it, and behind the cash register was where she was going to stay. Besides, in a few months it would be getting warm, and she would be back to wearing thin v-neck shirts. He couldn't have her wandering around the store, digging through shelves. She needed to be right where he could see her at all times. No, Mitch wasn't going to get any additional help in. That job would be waiting for Jim when he came back.

But something was wrong. Tinken's store had been going downhill for the entire past year, ever since that fancy new supermarket had opened up, but now even the customers who had come in on the same days for years were starting to thin out. Mr. Tinken's ledger, where he kept track of all his profits, began to see more red than ever.

No matter. Mr. Tinken had built this store up from nothing, he could do it again. He started by turning off the heat altogether.

"This is ridiculous!" Florence chattered from her position behind the cash register. "It's barely over twenty degrees in here! You can't do this to us!" It was the first time that Florence had challenged Mr. Tinken in all her years of working there. Mr. Tinken smiled. He was a force to be reckoned with, and she finally saw that.

"Do you want a paycheck or not?" he asked, putting as much suave into his voice as he knew how. "It's either your money or the heat. Something goes."

"How about something comes?" Mitch mumbled as he pulled up another load of cardboard boxes from the back room. "If you would just hire someone else, or close the store for a few weeks so that we could get caught up on unloading and restocking, then our sales might pick up some more. You know, like if we actually had a full selection to offer the customers when they come in to buy stuff."

Mr. Tinken did not appreciate the sarcasm, especially coming from Mitch the bitch. He was about to give him a witty response when Florence's voice quietly wafted through the cold air.

"We need Jim back."

"We do not!" Mr. Tinken fumed, finally feeling all the anger, the insult, and the unfairness cracking inside of him. "He left us without a word of where he was going or why! You act like he was a living example of a perfect 'employee of the month', but a perfect employee would at least give two weeks' notice. No, a perfect employee wouldn't even do that! He'd stay loyal to the company that has provided for him all these years! Jim Rines is a back stabbing, betraying excuse for an associate. We're better off with him gone."

Florence and Mitch looked at Mr. Tinken for a slow, quiet minute. Then Mitch picked his box back up and carried it over to aisle one to restock Mr. Blochett's cans of food. Florence quietly began adding more plastic bags to the rack beside her register, even though it was already full.

Good. At least they were keeping busy and keeping their mouths shut. Mr. Tinken didn't need their lectures.

But one thing that he did need was customers, and those suddenly seemed to be scarce. As if he could sense that Tinken's General Store was struggling, the tall brown-suited jerk at the mega supermarket declared a store wide super sale that would last an entire month. There was no way that Mr. Tinken could match those sales, even though he lowered prices where he could. Any customers who *had* still been coming were now lured away by the prices offered by Mr. Stupid Brown Suit. Finally the only ones who shopped at Tinken's Store were Ms. and Mr. Blochett. The entire rest of the day, from nine to seven thirty, the doors stayed closed. And a business couldn't be run on the sales of three cans of wet cat food each day.

Almost two months after Jim Rines had been late for work, Mr. Tinken closed his ledger firmly. It was done. Set in stone. The business could not survive without some type of massive loan with which to hire new people, get everything back up and running, and rework the store to somehow make it seem more appealing than that supermarket. And Mr. Tinken would not take out any loans that would be hanging over his head for the rest of his life... not to mention, the people to whom he'd talked about it at the bank had called his store a "bad investment". No, the time had come instead to close the doors of his shop.

Of all the reasons that the store was closing, Mr. Tinken could only focus on one. One worker, whose slacking off had certainly helped that supermarket gain the upper hand. He silently cursed Jim Rines, wherever he was, in whatever posh position he had abandoned them for. He hoped karma would find that bastard and punch him in his broken face. Maybe take out another one of his teeth. It would be nothing less than what he deserved.

Mitch and Florence were waiting for him by the front door as he stepped out of his office and into the main store. It felt like he was walking through a hostile land. The shelves were completely bare of everything; the items had been gotten rid of in a massive sale the previous day, which brought in more customers than they had seen in a long time. But it was still not enough to reclaim the business. They were behind in paying electricity bills, the scant heating bills that remained... nothing was enough to make those up.

Mr. Tinken felt cold anger fingering his insides as he stepped past Florence and Mitch, holding the sign that he had written on a sheet of printer paper. He solemnly placed it up against the glass door and used the last two pieces of scotch tape that were on the roll beside the register to secure it there. That way everyone who passed the doors would see the true reason for the beloved store's demise.

"THANK YOU TO THOSE OF YOU WHO WERE LOYAL FOR YOUR SUPPORT.
HOWEVER, DUE TO THE CARELESSNESS OF A FORMER EMPLOYEE, TINKEN'S STORE IS NOW OFFICIALLY CLOSED."

It was done. The death notice was up for everyone to see. Tinken's Store was finished. There was only one last thing to do.

There were still several crates of unopened and unused merchandise in the back, which Mitch had not been able to get to. Now the three of them would need to open them and send the things off to various places: other local stores who had purchased the items, back to the manufacturers for a refund, or to the dumpster that was waiting out back.

The work was begun in silence. There were only the dull thudding sounds of heavily laden boxes dropping to the ground as Florence, Mitch, and Mr. Tinken began to unpack the massive crates. If Jim had only been loyal to the company that built him, these crates of merchandise would have been going into the storefront to bring in more money, not being sent out in a last attempt to alleviate the final bills of the store. Mr. Tinken angrily exhaled, his breath fogging out in front of him as if he'd been smoking. He was positive that Jim had told the supermarket manager all about how the store was failing; how else would Mr. Stupid Suit have known just the right moment to strike and put them out of business? It was Jim's fault. All Jim's fault. Everything. All because of stupid, simpleminded-

"...What is-?"

The sound of Mitch's nearly breathless whisper cut through the cold silence of the back room like a scalpel blade. Mr. Tinken looked up. Florence was shuffling around the side of an especially large load of freight that was sitting beside a metal shelving unit, towards where Mitch's annoying little voice had come from. As soon as she disappeared from sight, a short screech stabbed through the air.

Florence was screaming at something. Mr. Tinken couldn't just ignore the situation, whatever it was. He dropped the box that he was holding, nonchalantly listening to the sound of glass crunching as whatever had been inside the package shattered. He dragged his feet, unwillingly carrying himself towards whatever new problem awaited around the side of the crate.

Florence had both hands pressed up against her mouth, holding the lower half of her face so hard that her skin was turning white. She was staring straight, unblinking, into a corner between the metal shelf and the wall of the building. Mitch was standing there beside her, dumbstruck, gawking in the exact same way. Mr. Tinken looked down at what had caught both their interests. He felt his lips part in a sudden gasp of shock.

"Jim?" he tried to say, but the word wouldn't fully come out. Jim Rines was there.

Or at least, what was left of him.

The familiar, lanky figure was lying against the concrete floor, wedged between the far wall and the metal shelves. He could have looked like he was sleeping, except for the fact that his skin was ashen grey. The features of his face were slacking, like those of the snowmen that the stupid neighborhood kids would build and which would melt every spring.

Jim Rines was dead.

Mr. Tinken couldn't tear his eyes away from the unexpected image. It seemed that Jim had been at the store for some time, as there were little holes in his clothes where the mice had begun to chew through them. Mr. Tinken felt his lip curling back in shocked disgust.

"What the hell happened?" Mitch said in a gasping voice that sounded like some sort of weird choking noise. He was almost drowned out by the "ohmygoshohmygoshohmygosh" track that was coming out of Florence's mouth in a repetitive stream of babble. Mr. Tinken blinked, staring down at the unmoving, refrigerated shell.

He remembered.

That night, the night before the morning when Jim Rines was late for work, he had announced he was going to stay late.

"Don' you worry about it," he'd drawled. "I'm gonna get some of this extra freight caught up on, an' then I'll let m'self out."

Apparently he'd never gotten caught up on that freight after all.

"Well," Mr. Tinken mumbled slowly, finally feeling life coming back into his numbed throat, "we'll have to change the sign."

DREAMS FOR MARIA

Little Maria had wanted a pet for as long as she could remember.

"Mama," she would say every year around her birthday, "will this be the year I can get a pet?"

Her mama, Maria senior, had the same response for her every year. With a shake of her head she would eye her daughter, reaching out to straighten the dark brown locks that never seemed to stay in their proper position.

"Little Maria, you are being a testa dura! Imagine, sixteen years old and you are still asking for a pet the way you were when you were seven! A nice Italian girl like you should be more worried about finishing high school with good grades, like your big brother did, and then finding a nice husband to settle down with."

"But I'm not interested in husbands, and grades are just numbers on a page," Little Maria mumbled as she pulled away from her mother's firm hand. "I'm so bored since Tony went away to college. I have no one to talk to now. If I could get a pet, it would help me keep myself occupied."

"That's foolishness," Mama Maria said, sucking a sharp blast of air in between her teeth. "You just do as I say. Pets are a waste of time, and they are dirty besides."

"But what if I just got a fish, Mama? A fish won't make a mess."

"I said no!" Mama Maria yelled, her temper finally snapping. Her thickly accented English broke into a slew of unintelligible Italian words as she stormed away. Why would her daughter want a pet? Little Maria was far too airheaded. She needed to focus on her school and her future. Why should she want to clean up after an animal when she should be thinking about cleaning up after her future children? Mama Maria couldn't understand it.

But only a few months later, Mama Maria found herself distracted from all thoughts of Little Maria's clever future when the girl fell ill with a fierce fever. Mama Maria suddenly found herself living for each present moment as she tried to nurse her child back to health. She didn't even notice that the girl's grades were going to suffer from the amount of time she had to stay at home, and then later in the hospital. She stopped wondering whether or not a boy would find her daughter pretty as the teenager slowly grew thinner and thinner. Now Mama Maria knew she only needed to make her child better. And she knew just how to do it.

"Tomorrow," she told herself as she stroked her daughter's hot forehead, "I will go to the pet store. I will buy her the fish, and it will distract her from the pain."

It was not the next day, but two days later that Mama Maria finally made it to the pet store. She walked in and immediately selected the two most beautiful fish that were available. Then she carefully carried the bowl out of the store. She didn't take it to the hospital where her daughter had been staying; she took it home instead.

Opening the door to her daughter's bedroom, she carried the bowl to the nightstand and placed it there carefully. Now everything was perfect, except for one thing: Little Maria was not there. Little Maria would never be there again. She had died in the night, before Mama Maria had ever been able to get her the fish.

Mama Maria sat on the chair in the room and gazed at the fish swimming majestically in their little kingdom. The fish that Little Maria had so badly wanted; that Mama Maria had denied due to a dream that was now never going to be. Mama Maria watched the orange creatures elegantly weave through the water, and she knew that all those years she had placed her love in the wrong priority.

"I am sorry Maria," she finally whispered. "I am so sorry."

THE DOLLHOUSE

An electric ding chimed through the thick afternoon air repeatedly as the car door opened. Carol stepped out onto the pavement and quickly snapped the door shut, silencing the annoying beep. Her blue stilettoes clomped roughly against the pavement as she walked up towards the open garage that was set at the end of the driveway before her.

Carol wasn't sure why she had stopped here. After all, a woman of her standing wouldn't usually be seen at garage sales. She was the vice president of a successful vacation magazine company, and could afford to be a member of any –and every– exclusive store that she chose. Even her socks had designer labels.

So why was she walking into a dusty old garage? Even Carol didn't know. She hadn't been to one of these poor people smorgasbords since she was a child, and this one wasn't exactly bringing back any good memories. Carol stopped once she was inside the shadow of the overhanging garage door, and cautiously wrinkled her nose in distaste.

Indistinguishable pieces of junk were piled high in every nook and cranny of the garage, while various dusty nick-knacks were laid out across two large tables as if they were precious cargo that deserved star treatment. Pieces of duct tape with the edges peeling upwards were clinging to the items, bearing large numbers that were scrawled on in thick black sharpie. Fifty cents. Twenty-Five cents. Two dollars. At least the owner of the sale was honest enough to know that their retail waste was not worth any substantial sum.

Carol walked slowly through the garage, her eyes quietly judging every item that she saw. Faded dress for a dollar, probably something that hadn't seen the light of day since the seventies. Foam Christmas decorations that were so gaudy Carol practically got a gag reflex just imagining them beside her posh modern home. Old stuffed animals with rough fur that were probably nests to thousands upon millions of germs.

And yet, Carol could not leave the garage. She could not shake the feeling that something was here for her. It was the same feeling that she had felt when she drove by the out-of-date home and had seen the misspelled "gradge sale" sign that was mounted by the mailbox. Something had compelled her to stop. Something was now compelling her to stay, in spite of the part of her mind that was screaming for her to run home and find a catalogue that only successful people like herself could afford to buy from.

But she didn't. She couldn't. She was here on a mission to find something.

But what could it be? It certainly wasn't that old souvenir cigarette dish that had dolphins and "ORLANDO, FLORIDA" painted on the inside. She was also positive it wasn't the white glass angel figurine with the chipped wing. After she'd scanned the garage three times over, Carol felt disgusted with herself. She fought against the urge to keep looking, the nagging little voice in the back of her head that whined for her to believe it. There was nothing here. Carol was just wandering around like another idiotic bargain hunter who couldn't afford to buy things newly made. She felt her cheeks flush with a surge of hot embarrassment. What would her coworkers say if they were to drive by and see her there? She had to get out of this garage.

She turned directly around, her shoe making a circular pattern in the layer of light dust that coated the cement floor. With her head elevated at a slight angle, she took a giant step towards the edge of the garage. She would right this wrong. She would remove herself from this lesser situation and never speak of it again.

That's when she saw it.

There, wedged between the old wooden construction horse and the plastic children's buggy, was a dollhouse. Not one of those plastic pink Barbie mansions that were advertised every Christmas, with the shabby elevator that always broke within two days and the cheap stickers that tried to make the toy look detailed. This one was made of wood, rising up three stories. The individual panels that lined the outside were painted a light robin's egg blue, while the windows, door, and steps were stained a bright white. Dark sandpaper lined the roof and looked amazingly like real shingles.

Carol quickly found herself next to it, putting her hand on the roof of the miniature home and feeling the rough edges beneath her fingertips. She hadn't seen anything this detailed in a long time. Her former disgust completely forgotten, Carol quickly turned the home around on its swiveling table, eager to see what the inside would look like.

It was divided into six rooms. At the very top was a small attic with a circular window and a trap door that lead down into a tiny bathroom. Two bedrooms connected to that, while the last floor of the home was divided into a kitchen and a living room. The bedrooms were each furnished with tiny four poster beds and wooden dressers, while the living area featured a couch and a miniature television. In the kitchen a refrigerator was sitting in the corner next to a counter, and beside that was an oven with the image of baking bread painted onto the wooden door. On the other side of the kitchen was a table with a magnificent meal laid out. Small plaster trays of ham, pasta, and salad were glued to the center of the surface, while a miniature plate with a tiny silver fork and knife were secured in front of each place setting.

Two dolls were resting in the little building, one lying on the four poster bed near the attic space and the other crumpled onto the couch in front of the silent wooden television. The one at the top of the house had straight black hair that fell in a long wave from her white head, which was missing one brown glass eye. Meanwhile the figure on the couch had an abundance of black curls that were put up in a stiff pile on top of her head. Her face was accented with thick lashes, each one individually attached around the rims of the large glass eyes that were the same color as those of the first doll's. Both figures seemed to be made of fine white porcelain, with jointed knees and elbows, and were dressed in faded gowns which probably would have looked quite stunning when they were new. Regardless of their current condition it was obvious from the detail work that they had most likely been very expensive at some point.

Carol stared at the little house, feeling a slight touch of disbelief. What was this doing here? Surely it didn't belong among all the useless nick-knacks and pieces of brittle plastic. This was a work of art, something that could even belong in a home as beautiful as Carol's. She wasn't going to leave without it. She turned, one hand still mounted on the scratchy roof.

Her gaze settled on the figure that was hunched behind a plastic folding table. Carol immediately felt a sense of disgust; even from this distance it was clear that this elderly person had not taken any time to color their hair or present any sort of good physical appearance. She took a deep breath and forced herself to leave the dollhouse, her heels click-clacking across the dusty cement floor as she walked up towards the curator of the cheap sale.

"Excuse me," she said loudly as she came to a halt on the opposite side of the table, looking down at the top of the silvery head. The rest of the shallow body was wrapped in a robe that was dyed a bright, cheap green. Maybe at one point it had been plush, but years of use had worn it down to a collection of stubby fabric and flecks of lint, barely held together by thin thread. Carol felt her tongue twitching, wanting to cluck in disgust, but she choked it back. This woman owned the dollhouse. If Carol had any hope of getting the unusual piece, she would have to maintain a professional attitude.

"Excuse me," she repeated, "how much is that dollhouse in the corner?"

The old hag slowly looked up at Carol, whose confident gaze suddenly faltered.

Carol had never seen any person who looked less like a person. The face of the woman was pale and saggy, as though her skin was barely maintaining its grip on her skull. Wide blue veins were visible just beneath the surface. She looked old beyond old, like someone who should have died a long time ago; a corpse that was somehow still breathing.

But the eyes did not match the face. Carol was used to seeing slightly clouded eyes in elderly people, reflecting contentment after a long life, or bitterness that old age was now upon them. Carol didn't mind that. That was normal.

But this woman did not have those eyes. They were a bright steel grey with a sharp spark in them; the eyes of a young soul, still thirsty for adventure and mystery.

"Oh, the dollhouse," came the reply. The voice that seeped out of the leathery lips seemed just as misplaced as the flashing grey eyes, sounding light and cheery as it bounced through the dusty old garage. "That's a very special piece, you know. For you, young lady... twenty dollars."

Carol instantly suspected deceit. A piece like that, with so much detail in it, could surely fetch more than a measly twenty dollars. And what did the old hag mean, "for you"? She didn't know Carol. Every fiber of Carol's experienced buyer persona screamed that there must be something wrong with the house; this old woman must really want to get rid of it for some reason. Carol glanced back over her shoulder, half expecting to see a nest of bugs or other such vermin crawling over the miniature blue siding. But the home still sat there innocently, half encased by shadow, no sign of deceit or treachery visible to the naked eye.

"Do you want it or not?" the woman asked. Startled, Carol looked back down at the woman. The grey eyes met her brown ones. For a moment, Carol couldn't speak.

"Uh, yeah," she stammered, feeling her professionally cool voice falter away in the piercing gaze of those eyes. "Yeah, I... I want it. Uhm... Please."

The old woman held out a thin hand with wide knobbed joints. Carol dipped her own hand into the side pocket of her white leather handbag and seized a twenty dollar bill. It felt incredibly light compared to the usual weight of her thick black and gold credit card. She dropped the piece of rough green paper into the knotted hand that was resting just below hers. The five fingers, each topped with a thick yellow nail that had been filed to a point, closed around the folded patch of green and hid it from view.

"Enjoy, sweetie," the woman smiled.

Carol turned around stiffly and walked towards the dollhouse. Bending down, she lifted it up at the base of its swivel stand and carried it out towards her car, being careful not to let any of the furniture fall out. Her arms started to ache almost as soon as she left the garage, but she refused to let the house fall, just as she refused to ask the old woman at the table for help. Carol walked, trying to force her heeled feet to take her towards her car faster. For some unexplainable reason, she felt the urge to leave that property as fast as she could and not ever go back. The very thought of the unusual old thing that ran the sale made her skin crawl. But that was ridiculous; what was she afraid of? That the old lady would be following her to her car? Staring out from the shadow of the garage with those piercing grey eyes? Carol took longer strides, eager to get to the safety of her vehicle.

It was a challenge to maneuver the dollhouse into the back seat of her tiny imported car, but Carol finally managed it. She quickly got into the driver's seat and put the key in the ignition, turning it more roughly than was necessary. She took a deep breath and flipped her long dark hair back over her shoulders before she allowed herself one last peep up at the house at the top of the driveway.

The garage door was now shut.

"Silly old bat probably had to go take a nap," Carol mused aloud as she put her car into drive. But even the sound of her own voice, resounding firmly over the perfectly tuned whirring of her car's engine, couldn't force the goosebumps to stop rising on her skin. Carol quickly pulled away from the curb and got back onto the road, heading towards her house.

• • •

As she drove, Carol suddenly realized that she would be asked where the dollhouse had come from. It was not as though she could just sneak it in past her husband, and if he found out that it had come from a garage sale, he would doubtlessly tease her to no end. She, Carol, who was probably the favorite customer of their credit card company, had stopped at a garage sale and picked up a deal from some local person who was just trying to make a quick buck. Carol shuddered at the thought. She'd often ranted at her husband about the stupidity of garage sales and internet bidding sites, which allowed people to make money without any real effort or talent. And now here she was, encouraging such cheating! She spent the entire way home thinking of excuses that she could use rather than telling the truth about where the used toy had come from.

Finally she pulled up to the large gateway that protected her upper class community from the outside world. Her car squealed to a stop beside the small guard house that rested in the center of the two gilded gates, which bore the word "HEAVENSIDE" at the top in all capitals. The guard, a short little man with more hair on his face than on the top of his head, nodded her a greeting and pressed the button that opened the entrance gate. It swung open and Carol put her foot back onto the gas pedal.

She pulled up in front of her house, a good sized home with a wide porch that was framed by two long white pillars on either side. The outside of the building was a blend of tan bricks and dark window frames, not too showy but just enough to remind everyone that this was a successful family. Carol pulled her car into the garage and shut it off. She got out and then opened the back door to pull the dollhouse into her arms.

Now, in the familiar surroundings of her own property, Carol felt slightly ridiculous at the way the old woman at the sale had given her the creeps. After all, she was just an old lady, regardless of how unusual her appearance had been. Carol was glad that no one had been around to witness the ordeal, and she promised herself yet again that no one would ever find out about it. With the dollhouse now clasped firmly in her arms, she made her way up to the door that led into the house and leaned against it, kicking the bottom of the door in place of a knock since her hands were full.

There was a click as the lock slid back. Carol could hear the sound of the door opening, but she couldn't see it from behind the blue siding of the miniature house.

"Well, well," said a slightly amused voice, "sorry miss, but we don't allow door to door salesmen here."

"Come on, Dave," Carol replied, slightly annoyed. Here she was, struggling to hold this thing up, and he had to pull another one of his jokes.

"Alright, let me help you out," he said. The weight was suddenly lifted from Carol's arms as Dave took the dollhouse and pulled it away from his wife, carrying it into the tiled hallway that led from the garage to the kitchen. Carol stepped inside and reached out to close the door behind her.

As soon as she entered the kitchen, she was greeted by a chorus of excited shrieks.

"Thank you so much, Mom!"

"Pwetty dawlhouse!"

"This is the most amazing thing I've ever seen!"

"I think this is the hit of the season, honey."

Dave had placed the dollhouse on the floor beside the kitchen table, and their two daughters were kneeling in front of it, looking over every nook and cranny of the tiny house with eager eyes that shone with delirious excitement. Carol suddenly felt her stomach turn and contract as she saw her little girls oohing and ahhing over the new toy. Somewhere deep inside, she recognized the feeling as jealousy. Jealousy that her children were playing with the toy that she had purchased.

Get a grip, she mentally reminded herself. *Why don't you want them to touch it? I bought it for them, after all. Didn't I? ...Yes, of course I did. I'm a grown up. I have a career to focus on. I don't play with toys anymore.*

Carol somehow felt that her own explanation wasn't adequate, but she couldn't admit that she had bought that house for herself. Especially not in front of her husband, who was now elbowing her and saying,

"Soooo... that's not in a box from Toys R Us. In fact, it looks a bit used. Don't tell me that the queen of retail actually sprung for a money saving deal?"

She recognized that teasing taunt in his voice. Dave was a big jokester, the life of any party. They had actually met at one, a college get together that had been hosted by a mutual friend. Dave's jokes had everyone in stiches except for Carol, and he'd sworn that he wouldn't let her be until he'd gotten her to laugh. Back then Carol had started to see the funny side of life with his help, but lately she had better things to do.

"I got it at a trendy new thrift store downtown," she lied, dropping her purse casually onto the counter as if the three hundred dollar bag meant nothing to her. "It's all the rage. The ladies in the office were talking about it so I figured I would take a look. The dollhouse made me think of the girls."

"Thank you so much, Mom!" their seven year old, Ella, repeated as she ran up to wrap her arms around Carol's waist. "It's amazing!"

"Ya, tanks you, Maah!" Tanya the four year old drawled as she joined her sister by grabbing onto Carol's leg. Carol stumbled backwards a few inches, thrown off balance. The little girls had no idea how hard it was to remain standing in heels, although they would learn soon enough. Dave was the one who had initially wanted children, but now that they were here, they were going to be polished to Carol's standards. Making a mental note to instruct them on how to properly thank people later, she brushed them off.

"Yeah, well, you know, only the best for you girls," she murmured half-heartedly. "I'm going to take a bath. Be back down in a bit."

"Dinner should be delivered by then!" Dave called after her cheerily, while the girls went straight back to the dollhouse.

Carol filled the enormous Jacuzzi bath with hot water, adding in a few of her favorite bath beads. It always felt so good to come home and soak after a long day of being professional. Her feet certainly needed it after nine hours of being crammed into tall heels. This was a rare occasion where she could be alone, to recharge and plan for the next day, and reflect on things.

No. Not reflect on things. What was she thinking? If she let her mind wander, it would surely go back to that one night, the one face that she had been trying to forget for most of her adult life. She would doubtlessly end up at that same realization, the one that she hated to face because there was no way she could fix it with all of her professional cool.

Carol quickly undressed and got into the tub to distract herself from her thoughts, but somehow the allure of it was all but gone. She got out after ten minutes and quickly pulled on a mint green dress with white polka-dots that was a little more comfortable than her work outfit.

The smell of Chinese food wafted up towards her. It was Tuesday, so Ella got to pick what dinner they would have, and she always chose Chinese. Wednesdays were Tanya's days for pizza and Dave, without fail, would order burgers on Saturdays. Carol always told them that she couldn't care less what they ate, as long as no one expected her to come home and cook. She was a vice president, not a chef. Dave was usually the one to cook, selecting from the book of recipes that Carol had printed out from health and nutrition websites the way that all her coworkers did.

But secretly, Carol liked the three nights when they were able to order in and it didn't have to be healthy or sophisticated. It took her back to memories of a different time, with other people that she had loved.

No, no, no! She had to stop going back there. This was twice in one night that she'd slipped off.

What is my problem today? Did that old crone really upset me that much? she wondered. Carol determined that she would keep her thoughts collected from that point on and marched herself downstairs for dinner.

Her husband and daughters were already seated around the table, scooping out rice and different chunks of meat that were covered in thick, sweet sauces. Carol took her seat as the three of them continued their discussion.

"There's a lot of detail in that house," Dave was saying. "If you girls were dolls, you could practically live there!"

"I'd LOVE that!" Ella exclaimed. "I would live in that big pink bedroom at the top!"

"But there are only two bedrooms," Dave reminded her, "and with the two dolls already in there, that would be four little ladies, so you'd have to bunk up together. Speaking of which, did you decide what to name the glass girls?"

"Yep!" Tanya interjected as she enthusiastically stabbed at a nugget of sweet and sour chicken with her plastic fork. "Dat one is Maah."

"That's right, we named the one with only one eye Carol," Ella elaborated. "She has long black hair just like Mom!"

"Hey now, how come I don't get anything named after me?" Dave asked in fake indignation. The girls both giggled.

"Cause you a boy, Daahd!" Tanya laughed. Dave shrugged.

"You could always name her Davida," he suggested. Ella roared with laughter, louder than Carol thought was necessary.

"No!" Ella finally said after she had calmed down. "We want to call the other one Kerri."

Carol's hand stopped moving, fork still clenched between her fingers. She stared down at the rice and sauce on her plate, trying to force her mind to think.

Kerri.

"Why that name, sweetheart?" Dave asked in a low, gentle voice. Ella didn't seem to notice Carol's reaction, because she buzzed on,

"Oh, well because you said it was the name of the lady in that picture that mom has!"

"What?"

Carol glanced sharply at Dave, who was clearing his throat uncomfortably.

"Okay. Well, girls, why don't we talk about the dollhouse later. Who wants more Mongolian pork?"

"Ooooo! Me! Me!" The girls chimed in unison. Carol tuned them all out, looking back down at her food in distaste. Her kids weren't even supposed to have seen that picture in Carol's study, let alone know any names. Carol herself hadn't seen the photo in years; she kept it hidden in a lower drawer of her desk. But she could still visualize it, a moment that was frozen forever on film: herself as a teenager, with an atrocious bob cut that did no justice for her hair or her face. Her arms were wrapped around the shoulders of another girl with similar black hair cut in the same style, only on her the bob looked sexy, playful, and sweet all at once. They were both wearing shirts that bore the name of some pathetic convention that they'd paid far too much for in the hopes of meeting a mutual favorite television star.

How did the girls see it? Carol asked herself over and over again as her family continued with dinner. *Why would Dave have told them? I thought he understood that I didn't want to revisit that again... I thought he knew how much it bothered me.*

The rest of dinner seemed to stretch on forever. Finally everyone had eaten their fill, and the girls left the kitchen to watch cartoons for a few hours before bed.

"You barely said two words while we were eating," Dave said as he stood to help Carol clear away the white cardboard boxes. "I'm assuming you're mad about what happened?"

"How did they find out about her?" Carol asked, trying to keep her voice level and calm as it hissed through her clenched teeth.

"Tanya snuck into your office one day when the babysitter was helping Ella with some homework," Dave explained. "She opened the drawer and saw the picture. They wouldn't stop asking me about it when I came home. I didn't want them to bother you, so I told them about her."

"What did you tell them?" Carol asked, taking a deep breath. It wasn't working; she wasn't calming down.

"Just enough to allay their curiosity," Dave replied. "Don't worry, honey. They won't bring it up again."

But Carol couldn't be as sure as her husband. After all, he wasn't the one whose stomach lurched every time he heard that name. He wasn't the one who had spent years in therapy trying to forget that face.

He wasn't the one who was hated his life.

There, she'd admitted it to herself. Her secret pain. She always tried to hide it; always tried to convince herself that she didn't have anything to be unhappy about. She had an attractive husband, big house, kids who got good grades, and was a successful career woman.

And yet, there was a gnawing emptiness inside of her, a desire to have something else that was out of reach. She was afraid to admit it to Dave, because she didn't know what he would think of it, and she definitely couldn't confess her unhappiness to anyone else. No one could know that professional, level headed Carol felt like she was dead inside.

"I'm going to bed," she mumbled.

"It's only seven o'clock," Dave replied. The usual teasing tone in his voice was replaced by one of serious concern. "Are you sure you don't want to talk about it?"

Talk about it. That sounded so nice, so simple, and so sweet. Part of Carol wished that simply talking to Dave about everything that was troubling her would instantly take all the problems away, making her happy and giving her that one thing that she desperately wanted.

The chance to say goodbye.

Carol shook her head and walked out of the room. She quickly headed back up the stairs and changed into her floral silk nightgown. Normally she loved to feel it sliding on over her body, cool and light and practically smelling of the expensive price she had paid for it. But tonight it felt clammy and cold, and clung statically to her skin. She quickly got under the padded covers and shut her eyes.

But she couldn't sleep. Now that she had allowed herself to go to that thought, that part of her mind that knew she was really unhappy, she couldn't get it out of her head. What could she do to fix this? What would people say if they found out that successful Carol was really empty inside? And if all of her accomplishments couldn't make up for the one thing she didn't have, what could?

It must have been several hours later that Dave finally came upstairs. Carol kept her eyes shut and tried to even out her breathing, hoping that he would think she was asleep. Apparently he must have, because he gave her a quick kiss on the cheek before rolling over onto his side. Within a half hour, his breathing sounded deep and slow.

Kerri. Happiness. Kerri. Happiness. Carol couldn't sleep with those two thoughts running through her mind. Suddenly, something else wedged its way in.

The dollhouse.

Carol felt another lurch in her stomach as she thought of it. The perfect miniature house with its two inhabitants, now named Carol and Kerri. Why had she ever stopped at that garage sale? What had made her so desperate to get that dollhouse? The more she thought about it, the more the agitation seeped in. It built up inside Carol's body until she felt it oozing out of her in the form of a fine layer of sweat that glazed her skin. What was so special about that dollhouse? Why couldn't she stop picturing it in her mind, wanting to go downstairs and take a look at it? In the darkness she could practically see the eerie grey eyes of the former owner of the house, sitting behind the rusty cash box. Carol felt nauseated as she remembered the woman. What was wrong with her? She'd seen plenty of people, young and old and in-between throughout her life. Why did this one lady bother her so much?

Finally, Carol threw back the covers and whipped her feet over the edge of the bed, putting them into her slippers and quickly storming from her bedroom. She'd never felt so confused, nauseated, and scared in all of her adult life.

Something's wrong with this situation. Something is just wrong. And it all started with that dollhouse coming into my life.

Carol practically flew down the stairs, her hand rubbing against the cold polished wood of the railing as she went. The living room was dark except for a few shafts of pale white moonlight seeping in through the windows. Carol didn't need light to see the way around the furniture; using her memory of the house she headed towards the kitchen, her pace quickening. The carpet from the living room ended in a line of tile underneath her feet as she reached her destination.

The dollhouse was still resting beside the table, a shape of darkness that was not reflecting the moonlight the way the white tile floor was. Carol knelt down in front of it, looking into the open rooms.

Everything was just as it had been when she picked it up from the garage sale.

• • •

Carol suddenly felt the sweat on her body turning cool, and she had to fight down an urge to laugh out loud. Did she really think that something was going to be different? That the lady at the sale had meant it when she said the toy was for her? That the dollhouse really had anything to do with her unhappiness problem intensifying that evening?

That it would somehow, magically, be able to fix her?

Carol couldn't believe how pathetically she was behaving. She chuckled to herself and pushed at the edge of the dollhouse, slowly turning it around on its swiveling base. She, a grown woman, had actually gotten up in the middle of the night and rushed downstairs to see if a child's toy had something to do with her problems.

She stopped the house in its circular motion, putting one hand on its side. The outer half of the house was facing her now, with the plastic windows glimmering slightly in the light of the moon. Carol looked it over, her smirk still on her face. It wasn't a bad find. Her girls had never seen anything like it before, so maybe the whole paranoia over the garage sale stop had been worth something after all.

Something caught Carol's eye. Something glimmered in the darkness, brighter than the pale luminescence provided by the moon. She leaned forward, towards the small round window at the top of the house.

There was definitely something glowing on the other side of the window. Carol hadn't pictured the antique looking model to be equipped with glow in the dark accessories. She swiveled it back around to the front and looked into the attic space.

There was only darkness.

"What the hell?" Carol whispered as she turned the house back to the opposite side, peeking once again through the top window. Through that side, the room appeared to be glowing with a gentle yellow light. Carol blinked at it, confused. Maybe she was just overtired, maybe it was just a trick of the moon lighting... but the room was definitely lit up.

Carol rubbed a finger against the outside of the window, and to her surprise, it swung open. She hadn't remembered seeing any hinges on the windows before. This toy certainly was advanced. She wriggled both her fingers into the space, trying to see if she could feel anything that she had missed from the open side, anything that might explain why the room had light.

She couldn't feel anything, so she reached in further. The only thing hitting against her fingers and palm was the wall; she couldn't seem to reach the floor. Carol pushed herself further into the house, trying to feel for anything that was solid and not vertical. Where had the floor gone?

Carol squeezed her eyes shut and pressed her body against the house, now firmly intent on finding where the floor had gone to.

• • •

Where is it, where is it? Why can't I reach the floor? Stupid short arms; if only I were taller like Dave. Wait a minute; arms? How did I fit my whole arm into the window?

Carol opened her eyes in a panic at the same moment that she lost her balance, tipping forward. She clenched her eyelids shut again as she fell, waiting to hear the splintering smash as her body collided against the miniature house, pushing it to the floor and breaking it into multiple pieces.

But it never came.

She opened her eyes and found that her vision was spinning. Slowly she pushed herself up, hands on her knees. She must have been sweating more than she thought she was, because her skin felt cold to the touch. Her vision came into focus. She blinked for a moment as she looked around, taking in her surroundings with a growing sense of panic.

Her white tiled floor had been replaced with dull brown wood. The room was no longer the spacious kitchen that she saw every day when she came home from work, but a dimly lit enclosure with an angled ceiling. The only decoration in the room was a small round frame that was hanging on one of the walls. Carol stumbled over to it, hoping that it might shed some light on what was going on.

It was only a picture; a detailed image of one of the dolls from the dollhouse, the one that had only one eye. But why was that doll framed here? And where was here, anyways?

The doll blinked. Carol jumped, and the doll jumped too.

Horror suddenly spread through her like a virus, pumping into her mind as she came to a realization.

This isn't a picture, is it?

It was a mirror.

Carol was no longer herself. She looked down at her body, terrified and transfixed all at once. The skin on her limbs and head had paled and hardened into smooth white porcelain, while her torso was made of a dark brown wood. A blue evening gown was sewn onto her frame, but one shoulder had looped down over her arm, revealing a gaping hole in the left side of the wooden chest. Carol raised her hands into view, examining them in disbelief. The fingers were all painted on and could not move independent of each other; she had the equivalent of baseball mitts for hands. She put them against her face, feeling the hardened features. Her mouth was frozen in a sweet smile, with lips painted on like a heart in the center. Just as she'd seen on the doll that morning, the right eye was missing. Carol felt the hollow hole in her face for a moment until she suddenly realized that she was feeling inside her own eye cavity. She quickly dropped her heavy hands back down to her side.

What was she doing here? How had this happened?

Am I dreaming? ...Am I dead?

• • •

No answer came to her thoughts, but a simple answer wouldn't have been enough anyways. She was certain that she had left her bed that evening, and she was equally certain that a simple fall onto the dollhouse would not have been enough to kill her. There had to be some other explanation.

Carol felt the panic still seeping through her body, trying to make her curl up into a tiny ball and cry. Could dolls cry? Carol realized that she might be about to find out. She put a porcelain hand against the side of the wall to steady herself; her head was spinning again and she felt as though she were about to lose consciousness. Something told her that fainting might not be the best idea as a fall could result in a break.

Literally.

Carol was just on the verge of blacking out when a thought crossed her mind.

Wait a minute. Wait! Doll or not... I'm still me. The realization strengthened her, and her jointed knees steadied a bit. *I'm professional. If I have a problem, I deal with it. If I was able to get three articles completely rewritten and edited for a deadline just last week, I can certainly handle this.*

She took a deep breath, and the fading edges of her vision came back into full view. Her head was still spinning a little, but she fought against it. Reminding herself once again that she was fully in charge, she forced herself forward, leaving the steadiness of the wall.

Her porcelain feet felt heavy, as though she were wearing shoes with lead inserts. She glanced down as her left and then right foot clomped forward, noticing that black shoes were painted onto them.

Apparently I can't even be a fashionable doll, she thought with a scoff. *Faded dress and flats. I haven't worn flats since I was twenty.*

She reached the tiny trapdoor that she remembered led down into the bathroom. She pushed the brittle floor panel aside and looked down. Sure enough, the room below her was a white walled restroom, complete with a bathtub, toilet, and mirror. When she'd looked at the house before, they'd just been pieces of china, sitting loosely in the room. Now they all seemed to be very real.

There was no ladder connecting the two rooms, so Carol had no choice but to swing her heavy legs into the opening and slowly ease herself downwards until she was hanging by her mitten-like hands. She stretched her feet down towards the ground, and when she felt them brush against the floor, she closed her eyes and let go.

As Carol landed she stumbled backwards, crashing against the sink behind her. A harsh pain cracked through her left leg, and she yelped. Placing her hand against the area she'd hit, Carol was sure she felt a small chip missing from her thigh, right where the porcelain met the wood. She glanced down at the ground and saw two small pieces of cracked porcelain lying against the brown floor. Nausea filled her.

I have to be more careful. Shoving herself away from the sink, Carol reached for the door and pushed it open.

She was looking into one of the bedrooms. It had a large four poster bed in one corner, with a thick beige comforter and some scattered toys set on top of it. The room was painted a gentle pink, and had several framed selections of dried flowers hanging on the walls. For one moment Carol wondered why she hadn't noticed all that detailing when she had purchased the house that morning, but then she looked back down at her unusual new body and remembered.

Nothing was the way it had been that morning.

Despite the fact that everything was new, there was something familiar about the room. Carol took it all in again and again, trying to pinpoint what was making her feel so much déjà vu. Little tremors ran through her porcelain skin.

"Hey, whatcha think of this outfit?"

The flashback suddenly sprung into her mind wide and clear: herself as a slightly chubby child in the eighties, dashing through this room wearing an outrageous pink feather boa and a worn-out red dress.

"Whatcha think, Kerri? Whatcha think?"

Carol instantly reeled, pushing the flashback out of her mind and looking around the perfect room with a sense of horror. How could she not have recognized it sooner? This was her old bedroom. It was almost exactly as she had left it when her family had moved out. All that was missing was the old Furby hidden under the bed, left there by Carol for the new buyers to discover.

I always hated those things.

Carol attempted to make herself laugh at the recollection of the electronic owl toy, but she wasn't even fooling herself. The fact that her old bedroom was here, in this dollhouse, was beyond disturbing. It was even worse than being turned into a doll herself. With her halfhearted attempt at humor dying on her own lips, Carol forced her thick feet forward as quickly as she could, crossing the room towards two doors that were standing side by side.

Somehow, Carol knew that she did not want to open one of those doors. She could guess what the next bedroom would look like: painted a deep velvety red, with a lava lamp emitting a slight glow from the nightstand. Posters of bands that her parents had deemed she was "too young for" would be mounted to the wall in uniform frames. She knew that behind the white closet doors, there was an array of teenager clothing that she had always envied while growing up.

It had been the coolest room in the world.

Carol reached for a knob, her glass fingers clicking against the hard gold orb. She took a deep breath and then twisted it, pushing the door open.

Relief rushed through her so quickly it almost made her giddy.

There was no bedroom behind this door, just a staircase. Carol had chosen correctly. She held onto the railing as she made her way down the stairs, carefully moving one foot in front of the other so that she would not trip. As she reached the bottom of the stairs, her foot clinked against the solid wooden floor.

"Carol?"

She froze, and everything froze with her. Time, space, life and breath... nothing seemed to move as Carol processed what she had just heard. She had experienced a moment like this before, when for a short period the world had stopped turning. That time it had been because she'd heard something else, something that had changed her life forever.

"Carol, come on in!"

There was no mistaking the voice, light and yet so full of command. She hadn't heard it in years, but somehow she heard it every day. It had become the voice in her head, the angel on her shoulder, which she had so often tried to force away. Carol was overwhelmed with the urge to turn and run back upstairs, to try to squeeze back out through the attic window the way she had gotten in. If she made it out then she could wake up Dave, and he would try to find some way to fix this. But if she was the size of a doll, how would she ever make it up the stairs that led to her real bedroom, where her husband slept, unaware of everything that was happening? Panic settled into her chest again, making itself quite comfortable in Carol's body as it filled her, and this time she couldn't seem to remember the words that she had used to snap herself out of it before. She could handle a stressful job, being unhappy, getting turned into a doll, and being trapped in a house from her past, but this... this was impossible. There was no way she could handle this. She felt all the years she had spent in therapy come crashing down around her as if each minute she'd spent learning to cope was a building block, tumbling down from the wall she'd built up around herself and burying her once again in a sea of despair and guilt.

Her legs moved almost by themselves, shuffling her glass body forward even though her soul was still drowning in fear and horror. There was an entry way in the wall nearby, with a flickering glow coming from it. The sound of laughter echoed in from the living room as a studio audience reacted to whatever scene was playing out on the television. Carol's hand brushed against the wooden frame of the entry way as she walked through, coming into the full light of the living room.

It was exactly the way she'd remembered it, with the white carpeting, cream walls, and one large brown couch sitting right in the center of the room. In front of the couch was the television, just a simple box that seemed pathetically out of date compared to the flatscreen that was mounted in Carol's full sized house. From the glowing screen came images of a woman in a tight miniskirt, with big hair and a loud laugh. Carol remembered that show. They had watched each episode together.

They.

Here, it was as if nothing had changed. Here, the past was still the present. It had to be. Because she was there, sitting on the couch in front of the television, her legs curled up underneath her while her hand was resting on the right arm of the couch. Carol looked in disbelief at the sight of that figure. She was porcelain just as Carol now was, with the same painted features and jointed limbs. But it was still her.

"Carol."

Carol jumped slightly as she heard the voice again. The other doll was looking at her as she slowly swung her legs onto the ground, pushing herself up into a standing position. She gently walked over towards Carol, her porcelain footsteps light and measured. Carol stared at the face as she came closer. Those were the same dark eyes and perfect, acne-free complexion that she remembered, with the thick black hair piled in an elegant updo the same way it had been on the evening of her senior prom. The dress that the figure was wearing was the same beautiful yellow jeweled gown that had been worn to that dance.

The figure stopped when she was only a few feet away. Her porcelain hand reached out and touched against the joint in Carol's elbow.

"...Kerri," Carol mumbled. It seemed to be the only word she could muster. Kerri smiled, the red painted lips growing wider as they spread across her face in a delighted curve.

"I've been waiting for you," Kerri said.

This wasn't real. It was just a dream. It had to be.

After all, Kerri, the older sister that Carol had loved, admired, and wanted to be just like, was dead. Carol's knees began to shake as she remembered back to the last time she had seen her. The last conversation they'd ever had.

"Gosh, Kerri, why do you have to be such a know it all?"

"I'm sorry, Carol, I wasn't trying to upstage you..."

"Every time I meet someone that I like, you always steal the limelight. You just have to be Miss Perfection. No guy is ever going to want to talk to me again, not after you had to show up to the rally and steal everyone's breath away."

"Look, I was just trying to do mom a favor by picking you up, and I didn't know being nice to your friends was against the law!"

"Next to you, I always look like a pathetic nothing!"

"Don't say that, Carol."

"I have to say it, because it's true!"

"Look. I said I was sorry, okay? Next time I'll wait in the car. And they weren't talking to me because they liked me more than you, it was just because I was a new person and they wanted to know who I am. Come on, Carol. ...Okay, fine. Don't answer me. Take some time to calm down and we'll talk about this when I get back from my night class."

Kerri had never come home from her night class. Carol remembered well the knock on their door at exactly 9:37 that evening; the tall policeman looming in their door frame; her mother's white fingers gripping the side of the door until her knuckles went from pale peach to white and then to red. Kerri had been making a left turn onto a road on her way home when she was hit by a speeding driver who had his headlights off. Whatever was left of Kerri was in a coffin that was glued shut behind a mausoleum wall. Not here in the dollhouse. There was no way. Absolutely no way.

"Yes, I'm dead," Kerri said, as if she had heard Carol's thoughts. Carol looked up sharply at the girl, as recognizable as she should be but still different, still china glass, still...

"A doll," Carol forced herself to whisper. "You're not my sister. You're a doll."

"Of course I am," she replied, as if that realization were the most obvious thing in the world. "I'm a doll, just like I'm dead, just like I'm your sister. Look, it doesn't matter exactly *how* this is happening, what's important is that it *is* happening. We needed to talk."

Carol tried to make herself become professional, to deal with this situation in the way that she had dealt with everything else, but the ability to be an adult seemed even further away from her than it had been when she'd seen the replica of her old room. The eyes of this doll were not glass, they were exactly the dark jewels that she remembered looking into so many times when

● ● ●

she'd been asking for advice, or telling her latest tween woes. She opened her mouth, the porcelain clinking slightly as her lips separated.

"I'm sorry."

The words were out before Carol had even thought about them, and everything else came with them. The guilt, the pain, the secret source of her unhappiness. The last words she'd ever spoken to the person that she loved the most were words of anger, of petty jealousy, of something that was never important in the first place. She'd toyed with the idea for years afterwards... had her sister been thinking about what had happened between them that night? Had that distracted her from noticing the approaching driver? Had it all been Carol's fault? She had promised herself that she would never again get close enough to hurt anyone, that being professionally calm and aloof would keep her mistakes from being repeated. But it had never been enough to make her happy. No amount of preparation for the future could make the past unwind itself. Nothing could bring Kerri back.

Until now.

Carol felt her body start shaking, the fragile limbs clinking as they knocked against each other. Water began pouring down the left side of her face from the one eye that she still had.

Stiff arms suddenly encircled her shoulders. Someone was holding her, holding her the way that she hadn't been held since she was a sniffly teenager in a drama crisis. The way that only her sister had been able to. Carol leaned her head against the glass shoulder before her. It smelled like she remembered Kerri smelling: slightly of her favorite lilac perfume, mixed with their mother's laundry detergent.

"I never meant any of what I said, Kerri," Carol gushed, stopping and gasping for breath. "I'm so sorry. I never got the chance to say goodbye and tell you that I love you."

"It's okay, Carol," Kerri said. She pulled away, holding herself at arm's length, and looked at Carol with a slight smile. "You didn't mean it. I know you didn't. You've been carrying this guilt around for a long time, and it's time you let go of your handicap."

Kerri reached out, her pale hand brushing against the hole in Carol's face.

"You've become so blinded by your guilt that you can't see half of what you have," she whispered. "Carol, there's more to life than just one person. I know it hurts that we were separated. I never wanted our time together to be so short. But you have a wonderful family that loves you so much. You shouldn't be blind to that."

Carol suddenly remembered the fact that she had a husband and daughters. She'd always supposed that they loved her, but only in the casual way that people who are bonded by relation always tend to. She'd never wondered what they would feel if she was not there; what would happen to them if she were to be taken suddenly out of their lives.

Or if they were to be taken from her.

"I... I never thought about it," she whispered. Kerri put an arm around her shoulder and led her towards the couch gently, seating herself and Carol when they reached it. The couch was made of a rough material but was still thick and plush, just as Carol remembered it had been.

"I know you've had a hard time admitting what was bothering you all these years," Kerri said gently, "but now that you've admitted it to yourself, I think you can open up about it to those who love you. You don't need to feel guilt over what happened to me, Carol. It wasn't your fault, and there wasn't anything you could have done to save me. We need to stop thinking about the awful way that we were separated, and instead reflect on the wonderful times we had together."

Carol's insides flipped over on themselves as she heard what Kerri was saying. Could she really open up and face the past after all these years? Could she really be free from the guilt that she'd been carrying in a cloud over her soul ever since her sister's death?

Kerri reached around her neck and took off a golden necklace. Hanging from it was a heart shaped pendant with black metal vines twisting around it. She had worn it the evening that she had gone to the prom, but after her death it had been given to Carol. Carol hadn't seen it in years, having purposefully let its location slip her mind so that she wouldn't have to be reminded of Kerri. Her sister was now reaching out towards her, and clasped the golden chain around Carol's neck. It clinked against her porcelain skin, with the heart pendant falling right down over the empty cavity that was carved into her chest.

"There," Kerri announced. "You may not be entirely whole again, which is alright, but now you can at least remember that it's not a weakness to love. If you look at life like that, you'll never be blind again."

Carol looked down at the pendant. Suddenly she realized that she didn't care what her professional friends thought of her. Suddenly it was far more important to go back home and tell her husband how much she loved him, and make her daughters realize how special they were.

"But what about you, Kerri?" she asked, looking back up at her sister. "Will I ever see you again?"

"Of course!" Kerri laughed. "Sisters like us can never be separated for very long."

"But when?" Carol insisted. "When will I get to see you next?"

One of Kerri's sparkling eyes winked inside her porcelain face.

"That's the mystery of it. You'll just have to get there when you get there."

Carol suddenly felt herself growing heavier. It was as if weights had been placed into her limbs, dragging her downwards. She fell to her knees, looking up at Kerri in a panic.

"What's going on?" she asked. Her mouth didn't clink this time when she moved it. Kerri knelt down beside Carol as the weight of her body became too much to hold upright, forcing her to lie down flat.

"Don't panic, you're just waking up."

"Was I ever asleep?"

"You were asleep for a long time. But now, it's the first day of the rest of your life."

Carol blinked. The cream walls were gone; she was looking at a large, blank white surface. Her fingers twitched. They were no longer attached together, and they were resting on thick padded sheets.

She sat up in a rush, her long black hair flying forward past the edges of her face in disheveled strands, no longer brushed flat against the sides of her head as it had been in the dollhouse. She looked down at her hands. Her fingers were a whitish peach color with perfectly manicured fingernails. Each one moved as she wiggled them before raising them up to feel the sides of her face. Her skin was not hard, but instead felt warm and soft to her touch, and she definitely seemed to have both eyes.

She was back. Carol looked around for a moment before recognizing the big white bedroom as her own. How had she gotten from the dollhouse to here? She looked down at her body and noticed that she was wearing her silk nightgown.

Was it all just a dream?

But it couldn't have been a dream. People don't change from dreams, and Carol definitely felt that something had changed. She felt lighter somehow, as if a weight that she had been carrying around for years had been physically lifted from deep inside her stomach. Suddenly the images of her husband and children flashed across her mind, and she felt her eyes widen.

I need to find them! I need to tell them I love them; make up for all the time I've lost trying to build walls up around myself.

Carol ripped the sheets off her bed and jumped up. The other side of the mattress was empty and the honey-infused scent of waffles was drifting through the air, which meant that Dave was cooking the girls their breakfast. Carol rushed for her bedroom door and yanked it open, not even bothering to put on her makeup or brush through her hair like she usually did. Instead she fled down the stairs so quickly that she almost tripped over her own two feet, cutting across the living room as she had done –or thought she had– mere hours before. She burst through the door to the kitchen, letting it slam against the opposite wall with a loud bang.

There were her daughters, sitting at the table waiting patiently for their waffles. She'd never stopped to think about how pretty they both were, having her hair and Dave's smile, and now, she realized, Kerri's eyes. Dave was standing behind the counter, a smudge of cream colored batter spread across his upper arm, holding a plate of golden waffles that had just come out of the iron. He looked up and gave her a smile for a second, but then it faltered as he noticed what she looked like.

"Is everything okay, honey?" he asked, his eyes glancing up and down over the image of her frazzled hair, makeup free face, and wrinkled nightgown.

"Yeah," Carol smiled. She had forgotten how nice it felt to really smile, allowing the muscles of her face to express themselves and not having to hold them back in order to maintain an image of professionalism.

She walked up to Dave and put her arms around him in a hug, pulling his body closer to her, smelling the rich scent of his favorite cologne. She hadn't allowed herself to be held for a long time, because she'd never imagined that anyone could comfort her the way that her sister used to. But she remembered now that she loved the sensation of her face against Dave's shoulder, the protected feeling that was washing through her now. She'd wanted to prove to the world for so long that she could handle her own problems and didn't need protection, but that no longer seemed to be of any importance. In that moment she remembered the way she had felt when she and Dave were dating, the love that she'd had for him and the way he made her feel special. Apparently that feeling had still been inside her, just waiting to be let out again.

Dave put down the plate of waffles and returned her gesture, wrapping one of his thick arms around her shoulder in return.

"Well, someone's a happy camper today," he said with typical Dave teasing, but his eyes were serious as they looked at her, questioning what had happened.

"Last night, I..." Carol started before faltering for a moment. What had actually happened last night?

Had it really just been nothing more than a dream? The more she was awake, the more it seemed to be just that. How else could she have gone down a dollhouse window, been turned into porcelain, and met her sister again?

But does it even matter what it was, as long as it happened?

"...I got some priorities sorted out," she finally finished. "I realized that I need to let go of some things that I no longer have, and appreciate the things that are still with me."

"Hey, Mom!" Ella said from the table, where she was pouring syrup onto her empty plate in anticipation of receiving her waffles. "You look like you just had a sleepover!"

"I guess I kind of did," Carol laughed as she walked around the counter and towards the table. That was when she noticed that the dollhouse was still sitting there, exactly where it had been at dinner the previous evening. For a moment she caught her breath as she looked at the little house, so different from the way it had appeared in her mind last night. The only thing that seemed odd now was that both dolls were sitting on the little couch in front of the wooden TV, their arms wrapped around each other's shoulders.

Carol knelt down and looked at them. The doll with the hair up in a bun bore no real resemblance to Kerri now, and neither did the face on the other doll look anything like her own. There *was* one noticeable difference though.

"Oh, you fixed her!" Carol exclaimed as she picked up the doll that she had associated herself with last night. The little figure now had two matching brown eyes fixed firmly in her head. Carol moved the dress to the side and smiled as she saw that a heart shaped felt patch had been glued on over the little hole in the chest, covering it completely.

"What do you mean?" Dave asked as he came around from behind the counter and placed the plate of waffles on the table between Ella and Tanya.

"I mean she's got both eyes now. And the little niche in her chest is covered," Carol elaborated. Dave raised one eyebrow as he stared at her.

"That doll always had two eyes," he said.

"Uh-huh," Tanya added.

"Yeah, I think it did," Ella agreed. Carol looked down silently at the little figure that was lying in her palm. She knew for certain that that doll had been half blind and heartless when she'd bought the house less than twenty-four hours ago.

Could it have been more than a dream?

Carol rubbed the side of her neck as she started to sweat. She knew that this doll had been fixed somehow, just as she herself had been-

Her fingers touched against something cold.

There was a chain hanging around her neck, a gold one that had something heavy on it. Carol couldn't believe it, but at the same time she knew what it was even before she pulled the pendant out from under her nightgown.

It was a heart shaped stone with black vines twisting around the outside of it.

"I haven't seen that necklace before, babe," Dave said as he put a waffle onto a plate and held it out towards Carol. "Is it new?"

Carol put the doll back into its house and stood up, accepting the plate that her husband held out towards her. She smiled and took her place at the table with her family.

"It kind of is," she explained, "just like I'm feeling kind of brand new today, too." She put one arm around Tanya, who was eagerly chopping at her waffles.

"Girls," Carol announced, "I want to tell you a story about a very special person that I should have told you about a long time ago." Tanya and Ella both stopped eating as they looked up at their mother. Carol smiled and continued,

"Let me tell you about your Auntie Kerri."

FAERIE

Once, I met a Faerie.

She was not like the kinds you see in books, with glimmering silver wings and little pixie ears. She was as tall as me, and she definitely had no glossy appendages rising from between her shoulders. There were only four very normal looking human limbs, along with hair that was dyed a shocking bright pink and which was instantly visible among a sea of black, brown, and blonde heads.

But I still knew she was a Faerie from the first moment I saw her. Normal people don't have so much confidence and strength of will that it shines out from inside of them. Only Faeries do that, because, as magical creatures, their souls aren't hidden like human ones. The pure essence of what they are beams right through them, without any biases or filters to mute it.

I was new to town, with no friends to speak of until I met the Faerie. She accepted me as one of her own and showed me her ways. With the Faerie there was always fun, always joy, if you knew how to see it. We would shop for pointless things, watch the people walking by, and talk about where life was taking us. I envied that the Faerie was so confident. So easy to talk to. So much fun. I always wanted to be like her.

I would later realize that she had troubles of her own when it came to fitting in. Although she had many friends and everyone talked to her, no one really understood her. They would smile to her face and then the moment that she turned away, they would talk trash about her. But I knew why. It was because they couldn't see that she didn't belong here in a boring world of pastel colors and nine to five jobs. She was a Faerie, and Faeries are made for the brilliance of the sunset, the freeness of the wind, and the adventures of the dark forests in the world.

The Faerie had been an example to me, but as time went on, I think I became an example to her, instead. Faeries are used to being free spirits, after all, but in this world, a free spirit can be drawn in many ways. Should she talk to this group, or that group? Should she be attracted to light, or dark? For a while we would ponder these questions together, and as someone who had always known where my moral anchor was, I offered her my opinions and advice.

But eventually, we started to drift apart. She was floating off towards new places, new challenges, while I chose to stay the same. That's the difference between a Faerie and a regular human, I suppose. She moved to another city; I started college. I began to write a new book; she got another tattoo.

I could only watch as she stopped trusting the instincts that had always guided her, and instead began to listen to the advice and opinions of lesser people. They pulled her down into the murk of their shallow minds, and she began to think as they do, act as they do, dream as they do. My voice was just another sound in the crowd, a muted one at that because of the distance that had grown between us. There was nothing I could do to help alert her to the danger as she began to lose her glimmer.

I couldn't stand to see my Faerie friend losing the spark of inner magic that she had always possessed, but I also could not change her mind for her. Faeries, like people, are unrestricted creatures and must therefore be free to choose their own paths. And if she had chosen to walk a dim road, I could not dissuade her.

Now the Faerie is little more than another human. Her majestic freedom has become anchored in lesser things, and as such she is now riddled with human concerns. I no longer see the glow of the supernatural around her, nor sense the sovereignty that was her wings. She is muted, her inner fire having gone from the brilliant greens of the deep forest glens to the pale mint of a confused teenaged life.

But regardless of how she has changed, having met a Faerie is not something that one easily forgets. I will never be the same since having been friends with her. She taught me to see the colors in between the lines of the world, to search for my own inner feelings and to express myself. With those lessons in mind, and the memories of when we were close, I found myself able to let go of the Faerie; to move on from the friendship that we'd had and accept that her choice to lose her Faerie glory might not have been what I thought best, but it was what made her happy. Able to conclude that while she was no longer who she had been, she had still touched my life in a way that only a true Faerie can. I will always remember her as that free soul with the glimmering eyes and colored hair, and I will always be thankful to her for the friendship she gave me.

... * ...

Last Christmas Eve, my phone buzzed as I was on my way home from church services. I opened it to reveal a message from a number I hadn't seen in so long, I thought it surely must be a mistake.

"Merry Christmas! I miss you."

Maybe the Faerie hasn't forgotten me, yet.

RING AROUND

-PENNY-

Penny had never been more excited in her life! On a spontaneous, romantic evening, her boyfriend of three years had asked her to marry him. There was so much to think about... the dress, the reception hall, the guests, the theme of the wedding, but first and foremost they needed to go pick out a ring. Penny didn't mind that her boyfriend had asked for her hand without actually having a ring present; she'd always liked the idea of the two of them picking it out together.

They'd finally found just the right one: a lovely chocolate diamond, nestled in a gold band and flanked by two white diamond chips, one on either side of the central stone. Penny kept staring at it with a smile on her face as she and her fiancé left the store. She couldn't wait to show it to her family, and most of all her little sister, who hadn't been feeling well lately and was in need of something to perk her up. Chocolate diamond was her favorite stone as well as Penny's.

"Damn! That was the last bus!" Penny's fiancé cried as they made it to the corner and saw a bus pulling away. Penny glanced up towards the sky and saw the sun sinking low. Soon it would be dark, and it was a four mile walk back to her house. She shivered, and her fiancé put an arm around her shoulder.

"Come on. We'd better get moving," he said with a sigh.

They walked together through the diming light, their breath making small clouds in front of them while the snow crunched underfoot. Penny glanced up, and out of the corner of her eye she thought she saw someone leaning against the side of a nearby building. Whoever the person was, they were tall and lanky, and had a glowing cigarette clenched firmly between their teeth. Penny watched as the figure suddenly seemed to notice them, springing up and walking out of the shadow to reveal a poorly dressed man with stubble messily glazed over his chin. Penny leaned closer to her fiancé and they walked faster as the man stepped forward to meet them.

The man came to a stop in front of them, blocking the sidewalk. Penny felt her heart hammering in her chest; something was not right about this situation. The man was reaching into his pocket with one hand while staring harshly at Penny and her fiancé.

"Help a buddy out?" he mumbled, attempting a crooked smile and revealing his nearly toothless gums.

"We don't have anythi-" Penny's fiancé began to say, when the stranger's hand came back up from his pocket. Penny stared down with wide eyes as he turned towards her.

Oh my gosh is that a gu-

-LUKE-

Luke hoped that no one had heard that. He hadn't really wanted to kill anyone. But what can you do? They were going to turn him down. Turn him down like the four other people that he'd asked this evening. No. No can do. This time, Luke was going to take what he needed.

Luke got down on his knees, careful not to get their blood on his pants. That would be a telltale sign that he had done it. He reached into the man's pocket and found a wallet. He took the cash and then shoved the rest of the wallet down a nearby sewer drain. It wouldn't do to have his fingerprints found on the murdered man's wallet. No sir, that wouldn't do at all. Luke turned to the lady's purse and helped himself to more cash. The purse was too big to go down the drain, so into the dumpster it went. Who would go digging through all that garbage? No one, Luke hoped.

He stopped and looked down at the lady. He had shot her first; he didn't know why. Now he was glad he had done this for her. She was immortalized now, her face frozen in pale beauty against the icy sidewalk. Now she would never have to be old or wrinkly, or lose her teeth like he had. She should be thanking him. They both should. After all, he could have let one of them go, but they seemed to love each other. Wouldn't they want to be together? Luke smiled to himself. He was a generous person, in his own way.

Just as he was about to step away, he saw something sparkly on the lady's little white finger. It was brown and gold and white, and more importantly, it looked expensive. He slipped it off, over her stiff finger with its painted red nail. Luke was no expert on jewelry, but he knew that if it was shiny, it was probably worth something. And this ring was definitely shiny. Luke put it in his pocket and took one last look down at the couple, lying red and white against the cold. He waved to them, and then set off.

Luke guessed that this ring was personal to these people, so he had to get rid of it quick. Thankfully he knew just the place. Pawn shops were made for this sort of thing. He quickly found what he was looking for and knocked on the door. The stupid fat man who ran the store was about to close it up for the night. Luke held up the ring through the glass to show him. Stupid fat man rolled his eyes and let Luke in, as if he were doing Luke the favor around here.

Stupid fat ass, Luke thought.

The man was even dumber when he talked, but he gave Luke a good price. Luke took his money and gave the stupid fat man the shiny sparkler, and then Luke left.

-JAMES-

James could have thought of a million other things he would prefer to be doing on such a blustering evening, such as listening to the radio while sipping a hot cup of tea. But here was some disgusting bum from the streets, and he had a ring that looked valuable. So James made the sale and then sent that bloody fool on his way.

James locked up his shop and took a closer glance at his new investment.

"A dandy purchase, Elliot!" he called to his dog, a stout corgi who was sitting on a padded red pillow. Elliot barked once in response, which James took to be an affirmation of his statement. He set the ring in a small black box and placed it in a glass case right atop the counter. Pleased with the positioning of his new purchase, James collected Elliot and headed into the back room, where he had his personal living quarters set up.

The next afternoon, shortly after opening his resale store for business, a young woman crossed James' threshold.

Very much American, James decided after looking her over. Her platinum blonde hair was mounted stiffly on her head, a testament to the hours of work she must have spent on it. Tight blue jeans and a black tank top hugged her curvy figure, revealing several tattoos around her midriff area.

Tramp, James thought to himself with a scoff.

"What a precious doggie!" the woman shrieked upon seeing Elliot, who was sitting obediently on his pillow. Elliot growled in response, and James smiled to himself.

Good show, Elliot, he thought, congratulating himself on raising his dog so properly.

The woman turned towards the counter and babbled something in a high pitched ramble, telling James about how she had won a significant sum yesterday at the casino and she intended to repeat the events tonight. Then she said something about needing a lucky charm, and pointed to the ring in the glass case. Without a word, James took it out and made the sale. She skipped out of the store with the ring on her finger, while James and Elliot had never been happier to see a customer leave their workplace.

-ELLY-

What! Could it seriously be that Elly was really this lucky all in one period of 24 hours? She'd never thought of herself as really lucky before, but this was, like, amazing. She'd won $700 yesterday in the casino, and that manager was totally coming on to her. She was gonna be married and living in a Beverly Hills mansion in no time. And this sparkly ring was her new lucky charm.

Elly made her way back to the casino ASAP. She was sure that she was going to get everything she wanted today, thanks to her new lucky charm. First, she'd win all the money in that casino, along with the continued promise of the manager's affections. After that, she'd get a boob job. Or maybe a nose job? What the heck, when she was rich, she could have them both! Then an even bigger ring than the one she got this morning, and a mansion with the hunk manager.

She escorted herself into the casino like she owned the place, because hey, she was so lucky that she basically did. Own it, that is. Elly made her way to the table where she'd played last night and got right down to business.

First round didn't go so well. Elly laughed it off and polished her new ring. Surely the next time she played it would go in her favor! But as the hours kept rolling away, so did her money.

"What is UP with this!" Elly yelled as she lost the last of the money she'd won the day before. "Come ON, lucky sparkle! You're supposed to, y'know, help me out here! You're supposed to be my lucky charm!"

"Why don't you make a private wager?" a particularly handsome gentleman said from across the table, leaning in towards Elly. "You say that's your lucky charm? Why don't you bet it in the next game?"

"You're on," Elly replied, flashing him a smile and realizing that maybe her luck would be winning the attention of this dashing man. Especially since her favorite manager didn't seem to be noticing her today, for some reason that she could *not* fathom.

However, when Elly was handing over her lucky charm less than an hour later, she finally understood that she wouldn't be getting that mansion any time soon, or the boob job, or even the stupid nose job! Not to mention, despite her loud sobs and wails of loss, the handsome man didn't even offer to give her back the ring. *What* a jerk.

"Fine!" Elly yelled as he walked away, slipping the piece of jewelry into his jacket pocket with a smile. "You take that dumb cracker jack bling! It's bad luck, you'll see!"

-LAWRENCE-

"Bad luck, huh sweetheart?" Lawrence chuckled to himself as he strode out of the casino and up to his black Lamborghini. He took out the ring and polished it against his jacket before getting into his car. "I'd say it's looking pretty good to me."

Hanging from the rearview mirror was a sparkling gold chain, the first expensive thing that he'd purchased for himself after coming into his cash. Lawrence had barely even known his crazy uncle, but he'd been more than happy to collect the massive inheritance randomly left to him when the man croaked. Lawrence took the chain down from the mirror and slipped the ring onto it before hanging it back up. He smiled at it.

"You'll be MY lucky charm now, won't you?" he chuckled as he whipped his car out of the parking lot.

For a few moments he was able to speed down the road as he was accustomed, but before he'd even gone half the distance back to his apartment he was forced to stop. The roads, which had been clear when he drove that morning, were now clogged with cars and traffic had crawled to a standstill. Lawrence laid on the horn angrily, screaming curses and insults at the insignificant nobodies who were cluttering up the road. The sight of all the rusty minivans and sputtering cars infuriated him; he was surrounded by lower class people and they were making his day a living hell.

Finally, the light ahead turned green. Lawrence rolled his eyes, wondering why it had taken so damn long. Slowly, the vehicles ahead of him started to move, and one by one they crossed the intersection.

"About time," Lawrence mumbled.

Without warning, the light suddenly switched to yellow.

"What!" Lawrence screamed, kicking the inside of his car repeatedly. "You call that a light? Screw this! I'm not waiting!"

Lawrence pressed his foot down on the gas pedal and his sports car squealed forward, moving around the cars and halfway up the curb on the right side of the road. The jealous working class people honked their horns at him as the light turned red, but Lawrence really didn't give a crap about it. He'd make it. The other people would stop for him; they always did. Why? Because he was rich and he deserved it, just like he deserved the money from his crazy uncle, and winning everything from that bimbo this morning. He deserved to make it past the rapidly approaching intersection in front of everyone else. Lawrence was going to-

Headlights. Honking.

-CATHY-

Cathy looked down at her brother with a sigh. He'd always been a reckless fool, and she was always certain that his craziness would catch up to him sooner or later. It was a bit of a shame that it had to happen this way, but oh well. There was no way to change things now; Lawrence was still and pale in his casket. The police had told Cathy and her family that he'd been trying to catch an intersection light, and had run straight into the path of oncoming traffic. His sports car was crumpled like a tin can by the huge truck that had hit it.

Good thing Cathy and Lawrence had never been close. She'd cried a little when she heard the news, but a full out crying session now would have ruined her makeup. And those damn little bottles were wicked expensive.

If Uncle Al had left the money to me instead of Lawrence, I wouldn't have to worry about that and I'd have tears to spare for this clown, Cathy thought with a sigh, pulling the wide brim of her black hat down over her eyes for a dramatic mourning effect. She made her way out of the funeral home, balancing on her seven inch black heels and pulling off her lace gloves to let her new ring catch the sun.

Not many things that had been in the car had survived, including her brother, but the ring and chain had been turned over to the family undamaged. There was a scratch across the stone, but a quick trip to the jewelers for a cleaning should take care of that. Cathy didn't even know why this ring had been in her brother's car, but it was hers now. She rubbed it gently against her jacket, polishing it just before getting into the passenger side of a well waxed car.

"You doing okay?" asked the driver, a brown haired man who looked at Cathy with gentle eyes. Cathy whipped the hat off her head and immediately pulled down the mirror to look at her reflection.

"Peachy, Jim," she replied sarcastically. "Just drive already."

Jim nodded quietly and pulled away from the curb. After a few moments, he glanced back at Cathy.

"What are you staring at?" Cathy snapped.

"That ring..." Jim replied quietly. "Where'd you get it?"

"It was Lawrence's. They found it in his car. Why do you care?"

"Because you're wearing it instead of the wedding band and engagement ring that I gave you."

"Well, news flash, Jim!" Cathy yelled, turning away from the mirror to glare at Jim. "That thing was tiny. It was like something you would find in a dollar store, for goodness' sake! I don't like looking like an imitation girl. I'm a real woman, I need real accessories. This stone is big. It's a chocolate diamond, which is much more unique. I deserve a ring like this, and since you didn't get me one, I got it for myself!"

Cathy turned her icy stare out the window, blocking out the hurt look on her husband's face. What, did he think those puppy dog eyes were going to win her over?

Not this time, sweetheart.

"I'm sorry you feel that way, Cathy," Jim was mumbling from the driver's side. Cathy rolled her eyes and reached for the makeup container in her purse. "And since you've been so honest with me," Jim continued, "let me be honest with you. I've been fed up with your crap for a long time, and this is the last straw."

Cathy glared back at Jim, snapping her blush container shut with a sharp click.

"Excuse me?" she demanded.

"You heard me," Jim said through clenched teeth, gripping the steering wheel and staring straight ahead at the road. "I always thought things would get better. I always thought that your harshness was just an act, and that deep down inside you really did care. But you aren't even sad over the loss of your own brother. You care more about the size of the ring I gave you than our entire marriage. Maybe it's time I found something new to love, too, because I certainly can't love a cold, heartless diva anymore."

Jim turned to look at her as he stopped at a red light.

"I'm going to apply for a divorce," he announced, blankly. Cathy stared at him in disbelief. Did this pathetic fool expect her to be upset?

"Do you honestly think *you're* ever going to get anything better than *me*?" she demanded, pointing a well manicured finger under his nose. "Well fine, go ahead and try! See how wrong you are. You're a scumbag and I don't know why I ever married you anyways."

"I guess it's mutual, then," Jim said as the light turned green and he slowly edged the car forward. Cathy mumbled a curse and an agreement, turning back to her makeup.

Turned out Jim wasn't the only scumbag who couldn't appreciate a real woman. That stupid judge who was in charge of their settlement gave almost everything to him.

"It was those damn eyes; he had to play up the part of the victim," Cathy muttered angrily as she kicked an unpacked box across the dingy apartment that she now occupied. But this was only a temporary arrangement. In no time at all she'd find herself a real man, a man who understood how to appreciate a woman who knew what she wanted, and Jim would be sorry. Then, Jim would look at her with his puppy dog eyes and wish she was back with him, but no way! She would never go back to that loser. He could sit in that heated pool underneath the back balcony of their old house and drink himself to death trying to get over her. But Cathy, on the other hand, would have a handsome bodybuilder on her arm, one who was taller than Jim, stronger than Jim, and knew when to keep his trap shut, unlike Jim.

In the meantime, Cathy knew she needed a little extra cash. As she'd very correctly reflected at her brother's funeral, makeup couldn't buy itself and it was *crazy* expensive. She glanced down at the sparkling brown diamond that was still adorning her hand. She loved the sight of it, but some sacrifices had to be made on the road to success. It was time to see what diamonds were going for on Ebay.

-SIMON-

"Nothing like a fool who parted with their treasure as if it were trash," Simon announced to the posters on his wall as he polished the ring, freshly removed from a shipping box. Superheroes and movie stars stared down at him from their colorful poses in a silent agreement.

There was an advantage to being a devoted online seller, and that was that Simon could recognize a deal when he saw one. Oh, could he recognize it. And to think that some people critiqued the way he chose to spend his days with computers instead of outdoors. Ha! This was one of those moments that really proved that his way of life was the best one. Some uneducated moron had sold this ring for only a half of the price that Simon would be able to fetch for it. Not to mention it was a local seller, so the shipping had been a few mere dollars. Pennies, really! Simon was practically salivating at the mental image of all the new gaming equipment he would be able to purchase after he resold this ring. He couldn't wait one more minute!

Simon rushed into the bathroom to run a comb through his hair, and then slipped the ring into his pants pocket and headed towards the door.

"MOM!" he yelled up the stairs as he pulled on his jacket. "I'm heading down to the pawn store."

"Be back in time for dinner!" instructed a firm voice.

"Got it!" Simon acknowledged. He winked at a poster of Halle Berry that was eyeing him from beside the door, and then escorted himself outside.

"I can't wait to show this ring to James!" he said to himself, adjusting his glasses carefully. "I do hate that stout little dog that he has, but oh well. James will be able to give me a good price; he has an eye for jewelry."

Simon put his hand back into his pocket to feel his lucky purchase, but it didn't seem to be there. He quickly stopped and reached in deeper, but there was nothing.

"Maybe I put it in a different pocket...." he mumbled, reaching into the enclosure on the other side of his pants. When nothing was there, either, he began turning out the pockets of his jacket, shirt, and finally his pants again.

Still nothing.

Upon a closer examination of the pocket he'd been positive he had placed the ring in originally, Simon made an unfortunate discovery.

"A hole!" he yelled, stamping his foot hard on the icy sidewalk. "MOM! I told you to sew this up, darn it!"

Perhaps the ring had fallen through the hole of his pocket and down to the ground at some point while he had been walking. Simon, after deciding that this solution was most likely the correct one, began retracing his steps back to his parents' house, scanning the ground along the sidewalk eagerly for any sign of the valuable item. But there was nothing.

"MOM, what have you DONE!" Simon yelled, finally accepting the fact that he was not going to find the ring again. He angrily kicked over a trash can that was sitting beside a driveway, sending the unpleasant contents spilling across the snow. Shoving his hands deep into his jacket pockets, Simon began to trudge home.

"I'll make myself late for dinner, just to show HER," he grumbled. A small, thin dog approached, looking up at Simon with big eyes as if he'd heard the word "dinner" and had understood it. But that was illogical; a dog couldn't understand anything that people say.

"Scat, mutt!" Simon yelled as he continued on his way, pushing his hands even deeper into his pockets.

-MUTT-

What was going on? Why was that person yelling? Poor mutt just wanted some food. It was cold. So cold. So hard to be a dog on the streets. People all around, but no people who were HIS people. No people who cared for a homeless mutt.

Starving. That's what mutt was. He walked with his tail between his legs. What was that? Did something move? Could he eat it? No, it was only a bird. Birds were too fast. Birds fly away before starving dogs could even get close.

But mutt could smell something. There was something here he could eat. His nose quivered. Garbage can, turned over! Old pizza crusts! Stale bagels! Bits of burnt chicken! His thin brown tail slowly began to wag. He padded forward. Tonight he could eat. Mutt scarfed down everything he could chew. Sometimes he didn't even chew. He just needed it. Food.

Something was there, between the old piece of pasta and the empty water bottle. It was sparkly. Like a collar, only smaller. One of the collars that people wear on their fingers. Was it food? Mutt sniffed it. It smelled like the garbage around it. That must mean it was food!

Mutt swallowed it, along with the old pasta. The pasta was better.

"Hey, there's the dang dog we been gettin' calls about!"

Mutt turned to look behind him at the sound of people talking. These people did not seem nice. They had a big white truck. In their hands were nets. Mutt recognized them. They were the people who chased dogs and took them away. Go away; he just wanted to finish his dinner in peace! They couldn't take him away, and they couldn't have any of his food! Mutt turned to face them, growling as fiercely as he could. But they had ropes. The ropes went around his neck. Mutt tried to stay, but they dragged him and put him in the car. The people closed a little wire cage in his face. Now mutt was stuck.

The car began to move. Mutt didn't like it. He began to whine. He wanted to let them know that he wanted to go back. He felt sick. His stomach suddenly hurt. Now he'd made a mess. Mutt backed into a corner of his cage and whined more.

-RUSS-

One more dang dog for the kennel. That meant one more thing for Russ to do now, but it was also one less dang dog to pick up later. He lost time, but he saved some time, too. Guess he came out right on top.

• • •

Russ didn't like being a dog catcher. Mostly it was because his job meant he had to round up those dang dogs. And those dang dogs were faster'n hell when they wanted to be. At least this one hadn't tried to run for it. After it was turned in, Russ could go home. And he was sure looking forward to that.

Russ got out as soon as his partner parked the van by the kennel.

Faster I get that dang dog put away, faster I go home, he thought. He opened up the back door of the van and looked in.

What a mess. Leave it to a dang dog to barf on the ride back. So disgusting. Well, Russ would have to clean the cage, because that was just how bad Russ's job was. Cleaning up barf from a dang dog: an all-time new low. Russ got the dang dog on a chain and pulled it out. His partner took it and marched it into the building. Russ waved after it as it left. He knew what would happen to it. That dang dog was gonna get put to sleep; he'd seen it happen before to mutts off the streets.

Russ turned to his job. He pulled the cage out and got a bucket of water. He turned the bucket upside down and let all the water dump into the cage. The barf washed away. That was that.

Russ was about to put the bucket back when he saw something. Something was sparkling in the cage. He bent down lower and picked it up. It was a ring! A real shiny one, too. It had some scratches, but it was still an interesting thing to find in a dang dog cage.

"Wonder if it's worth anything," Russ mumbled. He dried it off and looked at it as he walked away from the van. "If it's valuable," he continued to himself, "I can sell it for tonsa dough. I can get a place in a better town. I won't hafta be a chaser of dang-"

Something slammed against Russ. He was flying and then he was falling all in a few seconds. People were running. Everything was hazy. Someone was talking to him.

"Russ! Are you okay? Go call an ambulance!"

-RYAN-

Ryan was a firm believer in things happening for a reason, even if they were awful. He knew that that must have been why he decided to walk out of work for a quick breath of fresh air, which ended up with him witnessing Russ absentmindedly wandering in front of a car that was pulling through the parking lot. Ryan ran to Russ, who was bleeding where he'd hit his head but was still alive.

"Russ! Are you okay?" he asked. When Russ only gargled a half conscious response, Ryan turned to look at the horrified driver of the car, who was now standing behind him. "Go call an ambulance!"

The ambulance was there in a few minutes, and soon Russ was being loaded into the back of it and then was driven off. Ryan watched it go, mumbling a quick prayer for his co-worker's health. His phone suddenly beeped, distracting him back to the present. Ryan opened it to see a text message from his wife.

"Are you on your way? We're waiting for you."

Ryan quickly texted back an affirmative response and was just putting away his phone when he caught sight of something. He bent down and saw that it was a glimmering ring, lying there in the parking lot. Ryan looked around to see if there was anyone there who could have lost it, but there was no one else in the lot besides him.

What should I do with it? he asked himself. Almost as soon as he had thought it, he knew the answer. Ryan slipped the ring into his pocket and ran to clock out and put away his things. The mop, water bucket, and brooms that he used during his work day were securely locked into a closet, and then Ryan was free to go. For the other hours of the day he was just a lowly janitor at the local kennel, but now he was the most important person in the world.

Now he was a husband and a father.

Ryan made his way home and let himself in the front door. The smell of a homemade soup that his talented wife had no doubt whipped together wafted forward to meet him, but he pushed the hunger out of his mind and headed into the back of the house, opening a door at the end of the hallway.

The room was themed pink with purple trimmings, from the painted walls to the plush bed that was sitting in a corner. Rows of glass dolls stood stationary on shelves, with their porcelain smiles welcoming all to the room. Paper fairies hung on thin strings from the ceiling, giving the area an enchanted feeling.

But the face in the bed would have been anything but enchanting to anyone other than Ryan. Even he found it hard to bear, but his love outshone his pain at seeing the sight he did. His little daughter, scarcely ten years old, was thin and pale and pinched from her years of battling the terminal illness that had plagued her. Ryan had hoped that she would recover, but a recent blow to the family had hit her especially hard. Ryan looked into the eyes of his wife, who was sitting beside the bed, as he did every evening when he came home. Her gaze said the same thing that it always did: *we have her now, but we won't for much longer.*

"Hi, daddy," the little girl whispered. Ryan forced a smile onto his face and leaned forward to kiss her forehead.

"Hello, princess!" he crooned. "How are we feeling today?"

"Not good," she murmured. "I had a dream about her again."

Ryan looked away, and so did his wife. His glance fell onto the empty chair that was sitting next to the bed. It would never be filled again...

"We all miss her, princess," Ryan agreed quietly. "But she wouldn't want us to be focusing on that. She would want story time to go on, just like it has every night. But first, I have something to show you."

Ryan reached into his pocket and clasped the ring, hiding it in his fingers. He held his fist out towards his daughter, and then slowly opened his hand to reveal the piece of jewelry.

Her little eyes grew wide in her white face, and a sudden sparkle came into them again.

"Oh, daddy," she whispered. "Is that for me?"

"It certainly is, Princess," he replied, slipping the ring onto her thumb. She was so thin that it was even too big there, but she didn't seem to mind. She looked it over with a wide smile, admiring it from every angle.

"I found it in the parking lot of the kennel," Ryan said. "I think it was meant to be there for you."

Ryan's wife laid her head against his shoulder, and he put an arm around her. For a moment, they watched their daughter examining her new prize, happy as she hadn't been for a long time.

Ryan picked up the book that was lying in his wife's lap, waiting for him. It was a wide, leather bound volume of fairy tales, one that had belonged to his wife when she was a child. Ryan opened the book to the marked page and cleared his throat, trying his best to keep his tears back.

"It's still story night. Ready?" Ryan asked his daughter. She looked up, a smile still on her face, and nodded.

"I'm ready," she whispered. "I'm ready for anything."

His daughter might have been ready for anything, but even knowing that it was coming was no comfort to Ryan when his princess died quietly in her sleep a few nights later. The coroners had come and gone, and now Ryan and his wife were left holding only each other, staring silently at the empty chair next to the now-empty bed.

Ryan kept reminding himself that everything happens for a reason, but the words felt hollow and pointless as he watched a little white casket being lowered into the cold ground one bleak morning. Inside that casket was the body of his little princess, wearing her favorite glittery party dress, her golden curls perfectly arranged on the silken pillows, and with her new ring still mounted on her finger. Ryan would never see her again; her body now belonged to the deep black hole that she was being tucked into. Next to it were two other grave plots, which had been covered not long ago. Ryan quietly walked up to one of them and knelt down before it.

Tears stung his eyes as he read the inscription on the marker and tried to grasp that she was really here. His older daughter, so ready to take on life and so incredibly happy, was underneath the ground. And now, so was his princess.

"She never got over losing you," he whispered. "None of us ever will. I think she wanted to be with you more than with us. But in a way, it was almost as if you were still here, to help her at the end. She smiled like she hadn't smiled since before we lost you."

Ryan reached out and touched the name on the gravestone gently before rising to his feet. He looked over at the burial spot for his princess, where his wife was standing alone, sobbing into the ground that covered her youngest child. Ryan glanced back down at the gravestone in front of him.

"Take care of her, Penny," he whispered.

RENEE MARIE PHILOMENA THÉRÈSE KRAY

lives in Michigan in a house at the end of a dead end dirt road with her parents, eight siblings, and one really dumb dog. Having been homeschooled through elementary and high school, she was able to experiment with writing from a young age and quickly fell in love with the art.

A screen and stage writer for years, THINK AGAIN is Renee's first venture into short stories. Upcoming projects include an illustrated novel for adults, a graphic novel, and several full length novels.

www.facebook.com/HomburgerPublications

www.rmptk.webs.com

JEREMY JAYME

is, indeed, a girl with a guy name and is in every way "cool with it".

She is an artist with an ongoing love affair with storytelling. Her mind is never used to staying in one place. The inconsistency and adventure of film and the creation of stories (each project never the same) gives her this satisfaction. She uses her self-taught drawing powers to bring scenes/characters to life.

Jeremy frequently collaborates with her twin sister, Jemely, in various visual storytelling projects that they release under Dead Wringer Productions: the business they founded/own together. She currently resides in Washington state.

www.deadwringerproductions.com
www.facebook.com/jaymetwins.art

LIZZI PETERS

is a college graduate currently identified as a starving artist. She lives in a small town in Michigan with her very spoiled cat. Being homeschooled through junior high and high school, she was able to more fully develop her talents by applying art in all of her studies.

THINK AGAIN is the first work that Lizzi has professionally illustrated. Her love for music, nature, poetry, pop culture, and all things "different" are her biggest sources of inspiration for her artwork.

www.leadpoison.co.nf

• • •

ACKNOWLEDGMENTS

This collection is dedicated to my grandparents, who inspired me with their life stories as I was just starting to write my own.

The author would like to thank:

Rick, Nicki, and Deanna Kray (and I guess the bros and the Skoosh as well)
for their feedback, support, and general all around awesomeness.

Jemely and Jeremy Jayme
for being my Xenas.

Lizzi Peters
for allowing me to feature your work and for being the best other me that I could want.

Sharon Cicilian
for encouraging me to take the next step in the writing world.

Marie Masters
for being the best writing mentor I could have ever asked for.

(l)8D
Homburger Publications

www.ingramcontent.com/pod-product-compliance
Lightning Source LLC
Chambersburg PA
CBHW071301130626
46556CB00003B/1420